"There's the baby."

Of course, Leigh thought. "That's not good enough. I don't need a husband just because I'm pregnant."

"We find each other sexy as hell." Nick's voice was a low growl.

"That's true," she said with a nervous laugh. "One touch from you and I can't think."

"Is that so bad?" He reached for her, but she stepped back.

"For me it is. I don't trust my judgement anymore."

"And he didn't help any."

"He?"

Nick gestured towards her middle. "The guy who got you pregnant, then disappeared."

Good grief, Leigh thought. How could she have forgotten that Nick didn't know that he was the baby's father...?

Dear Reader,

It's the moment you've all been waiting for, the publication of the 1000th Silhouette Desire®. It's Diana Palmer's *Connal*, the next title in her terrific TEXAN LOVERS mini-series. Diana was one of the very first Desire writers, and her many wonderful contributions to the line have made her one of our most beloved authors. This story is sure to make its way to your shelf of 'keepers'.

And there's so much more! Don't miss *Baby Dreams*, the first book in a fabulous new series, THE BABY SHOWER, by Raye Morgan. Award-winning author Jennifer Greene also starts a new mini-series, THE STANFORD SISTERS, with the delightful *The Unwilling Bride*. For something a little different, take a peek at Joan Elliott Pickart's *Apache Dream Bride*. And the fun keeps on coming with Judith McWilliams' *Instant Husband*, the second in THE WEDDING NIGHT series. Last, but by no means least, we've got promising new author Amanda Kramer's charming and sexy *Baby Bonus*.

What a line-up! And that's not all, because if you turn to the end pages you'll find your chance to win a year's worth of Silhouette Desire novels—absolutely FREE! We know you'll enjoy our celebration month. Long may the passion continue!

Sincerely,

The Editors

Baby Bonus
AMANDA KRAMER

SILHOUETTE
Desire

First published in Great Britain 1996 Silhouette Books, Eton House, 18-24 Paradise Road, Richmond, Surrey TW9 1SR

© Jacqueline A. Bielowicz 1996

ISBN 0 373 76002 7

22-9610

Printed and bound in Great Britain by Mackays of Chatham PLC, Chatham

I dedicate this book to the Vicious Circle, Nag-Masters of the Universe and with special thanks to those who were there from the beginning, Debby Camp, Joyce Anglin and Susan Atherton.

AMANDA KRAMER

fell in love with reading when she was three, romance novels when she was eight, and writing fiction when she was ten, so it's not surprising she is now a published author, writing her own romances. Between the ages of ten and "mumble-mumble", she raised two sons, worked as a paediatric nurse and scribbled furiously in her spare time. Now she lives alone except for a demented dog, brain-burned cat, bewitched computer and twelve sexy heroes, all clamouring for her to tell their stories.

Dear Reader,

The excitement never ends! Silhouette Desire® has long been my favourite romance line, and when they asked to publish my first novel, *Baby Bonus*, I was in seventh heaven. After all, I would be joining Diana Palmer, Joan Hohl, Elizabeth Lowell and other very talented ladies who had given me hours of reading pleasure. Then my editor told me my book would be part of the celebration for Desire's 1000th title. One thousand tales of love and commitment, passion and heartbreak, and I have the chance to pay tribute to them. To all the staff at Silhouette, I congratulate you, and wish you a thousand more. As for me, life doesn't get any better than to become part of the Desire family!

Amanda Kramer

One

Leigh Townsend wondered how a man as good-looking as Nicholas Romano could be such a pain in the butt. She thoughtfully sipped her champagne and watched her tall, dark and impossible boss gesture to a waiter behind the buffet. Even from across the crowded room she could tell Nick was asking the man for more raw vegetables. Leigh chuckled, then took another sip of her wine. Fine with her. That left more petits fours for everyone else.

"Having fun?"

Leigh smiled at Maggie Kingman as the plump, white-haired woman, dressed in a bright red blouse with a holly leaf design and long black velvet skirt, slipped into the chair next to her and started nibbling from a plateful of munchies.

"Yes. I'm glad you talked me into coming," Leigh said.

"I know this is a bad time for you, your first Christmas since your folks died. But staying home alone would just make it harder."

Grief stabbed through Leigh's chest at the memory of her parents, who'd died in a fire at their rural home the previous August. She took a deep breath to ease the tightening in her throat. "I've never spent a Christmas without them, even when I was married," she whispered. "I really miss them. I can't believe I won't be with them for Christmas next week."

Maggie patted Leigh's hand. "I know. The secret is to hold the memories, while you build new traditions. And believe me, this office party is a good start."

Leigh pushed aside her sadness and forced her attention back to the bright, noisy crowd in the hotel ballroom. "I didn't know what I was missing, skipping the party every year to get an early start home. Does Marilyn always bring those awful cookies?"

"Yes, and I think she freezes the leftovers every year. At least, they seem to get worse each year. Oh, and stay away from the punch. Bob Patterson spiked it."

"Thanks for the warning." Leigh gestured with her glass. "I'm drinking my first champagne and I love it! I'll probably stick to the bubbly."

"Don't forget you're driving."

"No, I'm not. I don't like traveling late at night, so I checked into the hotel for tonight. I promise I'm keeping track, Maggie. I may be a little tipsy, but not enough to keep me from enjoying myself."

The other woman looked doubtful. "Hmm."

"Besides, it's not me you should be warning about the punch." Leigh laughed as she gestured toward the bowl. "I've seen Nick dipping into the bowl several times."

"Oh, no. He seldom drinks. I'd better—"

"C'mon, Maggie. Stop mothering everyone. Wouldn't you like to see Mr. Health Nut get wild for a change?"

Maggie looked at her in surprise. "I thought you liked Nick."

Leigh shrugged. "I do. As a boss, anyway. Let's face it, though, he does tend to go overboard on the health jazz. I mean, no smoking at my own desk, decaf coffee . . ." She cocked her head toward Maggie. "And his idea of Christ-

mas gifts? Be honest, Maggie. Wouldn't you really rather
have the box of chocolates your boss gave you than the
tofu, wheat germ and bee pollen Nick gave me?''

"Yes," Maggie said with a chuckle. "But I've heard you
during coffee break. You sounded mighty attracted, tofu
and all."

Leigh grinned back to her. "Okay, okay. I admit he's
gorgeous, but that's as far as it goes. We don't exactly have
a lot in common, do we?"

"I think you have more in common than you realize,"
Maggie said as she glanced across the room. "Uh-oh. I see
a wallflower in the making. I need to find her a partner."

Leigh shook her head as Maggie darted away. It always
amazed her how Maggie kept track of everyone. She rose,
walked to the cash bar, and signaled for a refill on her
champagne. While she waited, she scanned the colorful
crowd. The annual Christmas party for Kiefer and
Romano, Attorneys-at-Law, was in full swing. A tall
Christmas tree, trimmed with twinkling lights and old-
fashioned decorations, dominated the crowded room. Ef-
fervescence bubbled through Leigh like the champagne in
her glass as her body swayed to the music of the live band.

Through a break in the gathering, she spotted Nick in a
corner, talking to Andrew Kiefer, the senior partner. Remembering Maggie's warning, she muffled a chuckle when
she saw the cup of punch in Nick's hand.

The potent liquid had done him a lot of good, she
thought. She noticed his tie was missing, and his hair
looked as if he had run his fingers through it more than
once. She hadn't seen him this relaxed in the two years
she'd worked for him, not even at the annual company
picnic. Yes, he definitely looked different from the yuppie
she saw each day in the office.

Sipping her wine, she let her gaze skim over him. She had
to admit she liked that sense of primitive male under the
custom-tailored suit. With his broad shoulders and wide
chest tapering to a narrow waist and lean hips, he looked as
solid as a massive oak tree. She definitely agreed with office gossip that he was every woman's definition of a hunk.

When she saw him looking at her, her breath caught in her throat. He walked across the room toward her, and she was unable to break away from his magnetic stare. Vaguely aware the band was playing a slow, dreamy number, it seemed natural to step into his open arms.

"I've been waiting for this moment all evening," he drawled, smiling into her eyes. His voice rumbled from deep in his broad chest and warmed her like a dark, rich wine.

She smiled up at him and let her gaze wander over his craggy features. He had a wide forehead and slightly crooked nose. She wondered if Nick could claim a Roman centurion among his Italian ancestors. His mouth was full and sensual with a tiny scar in one corner that she suddenly wanted to taste. She blinked her eyes and swallowed hard.

He chuckled. "Go ahead. You can kiss it."

Startled, she gazed up at him. She couldn't believe this was Nick Romano, her uptight boss. His expression danced with mischief, daring her. She hesitated. Then, never one to pass up a dare, provocatively kissed the small mark, just brushing it with the tip of her tongue. A tingle swept through her as he drew in a sharp breath. His arm tightened around her waist, and with a swift, graceful movement, he had her tucked into a dimly lit alcove. His brown eyes, so dark they appeared black, narrowed, and his nostrils flared.

"You look like a naughty Christmas angel in that red dress," he murmured.

The heat of his hand surged up her back like a brand.

"Naughty? Does that mean I won't get what I want for Christmas?" Leigh's heart thumped with excitement. Was this really her? Flirting with the man she had always considered stuffy? But the Nick holding her now wasn't stuffy. Not at all. In fact, she couldn't remember when she had felt so...so feminine.

"Oh, I think I can promise you'll get what you want." His head bent toward her, and she waited in breathless anticipation.

"May I cut in?"

Disappointed, Leigh looked up and saw Andrew Kiefer tapping Nick's shoulder. She glanced back at Nick and saw him wink at her.

"No, Drew. I'm keeping this angel for myself," Nick said in a firm tone.

Leigh laughed softly as Nick whirled her away, leaving the usually verbose Drew speechless.

"Now, where were we?" he whispered as he nuzzled her ear.

"You were promising me I'd get what I wanted for Christmas."

"Yes, we'll have to see what old Santa brings, won't we?" Nick's words were soft, slightly slurred.

"You mean I might get something nice in my stocking?"

Nick chuckled. "I've been watching you all evening, angel. You already have something nice in your stockings. In fact, I'd even say you have something spectacular in them."

Heat rushed up Leigh's throat and over her cheeks. It tingled along her body like sheet lightning.

Nick arched one eyebrow. "A blush? I didn't think anything could fluster you, angel."

Leigh wanted to respond—say something, anything—but the thought of Nick watching her legs all evening seemed to have frozen her brain. She felt her blush deepen and Nick laughed.

"I'd better stop teasing you, or I'll be putting my own Christmas stocking in peril."

Leigh chuckled. "Yes, it's too close to Christmas. You wouldn't want to risk Santa crossing you off his list, would you?"

"I wonder if it wouldn't be worth it," Nick murmured, his eyes narrowing in speculation.

Leigh was glad the music ended at that moment, because she had no idea what she would have said. Maybe it was the wine, or maybe it was the season, but Leigh felt as if she'd entered a whole new world. One thing was for sure. She didn't recognize herself . . . or Nick.

The rest of the evening passed like a surrealistic dream. Colors shimmered as if touched by crystal. Leigh and Nick mingled, but Leigh was always aware of his warm, possessive touch. She knew she was responding to the comments around her, but all she really heard was his voice.

She had never seen him so relaxed. In the office she had always respected his commanding presence and admired his brilliant mind—cool and razor sharp. But tonight she saw him as charming and witty. She knew she would never see him in the same coldly professional role again.

For her, the best part of the evening was when she was on the dance floor, locked in Nick's arms, held tightly against his hard body. Then she was isolated from the crowd, lost in the spell he was weaving. His normally stern expression softened with promise. His scent of soap and wool and man surrounded her like a heady bouquet. She closed her eyes and laid her cheek against his shoulder, her head tucked under his chin. His lips brushed over her hair and she sighed with contentment.

As far as she was concerned, this magic evening could last forever.

"Hi-ho, Silver, awa-aa-y!"

Leigh Townsend opened her eyes, then closed them against the harsh light. The pounding William Tell Overture matched the throbbing in her head. Where was she? Wherever she was, she had had too short a night, and her aching head was letting her know. She ran her dry tongue over fuzzy teeth and grimaced. Lord, she wished she had the strength to make it to the bathroom, but every muscle in her body hurt. And why was there an orchestra in the room?

She looked for the source of the obscene noise and spotted a television in the corner of the room. A mad swirl of color on the screen splashed the message that America's favorite bubblegum was available to make her the most sought-after sex object of every male teenybopper in town.

Leigh groaned and closed her eyes. Oh, God. Not now. How could she face this kind of insanity when her head hurt so much? She forced her eyes open again, and her gaze fell on the remote control bolted to the nightstand next to the bed. She fumbled for the Off button, and blessed silence fell over the room. She sighed briefly in relief. Now, maybe she could think. To start with, where the hell was she?

She cautiously eased open her eyelids, relieved to find the dim light didn't hurt her eyes. She scanned as much of the area as she could without moving. Everything was hotel bland, she thought, but what hotel? She licked her dry lips as her fragmented memory slowly came together.

The Christmas party. Yes, last night had been the office Christmas party. It had been held at the Doubletree Hotel in downtown Tulsa, and she had checked in, hadn't she? So she must be in her room. She flinched as another shard of pain cut through her head. If this was what champagne did to a person, she'd stick with beer from now on. Her eyes drifted shut at the thought. Now, if she could only get back to sleep.

She wiggled further under the sheet. A heavy, warm weight dropped across her waist and she froze. Her eyelids flew open, and she saw a man's arm resting across her middle. What the...? Panic clutched her throat, her gaze darting around the room as she frantically searched for clues.

Oh, God, what had she done? She forcibly calmed her rapid breathing. She'd only had one lover in her life, and she'd been married to him. So, it wasn't likely she'd let herself be picked up, was it? There had to be a logical reason why she was in bed with some man. All she had to do was identify her unknown bed partner and she'd have that reason. Right?

Trying to ignore her headache, Leigh peeked over her shoulder at the sleeping man. For a second she didn't recognize the rough-hewn face. Her gaze wandered over the dark hair tousled on his forehead, the hollow cheeks shadowed by early-morning stubble. *Ohmigod, it's Nick!*

She buried her face in her pillow, searching in her swirling thoughts for answers. She remembered them dancing, but how had she ended up in bed with her boss? She glanced at Nick, noticing mistletoe scattered on the bed and, in one surge, the puzzle pieces fell into place.

She relived how Nick had insisted on escorting her to her room, then demanded one more dance. Since they could no longer hear the band, they had danced to the music of the late-night show on the television. Rack her brains as she would, she couldn't remember the name of the movie. She could only recall Nick pulling a bedraggled piece of mistletoe from his pocket and holding it over her head. As if he had needed mistletoe to tempt her, when his kisses made her feel so wild.

She turned on her side, careful not to awaken him, and surveyed the slumbering man. He might not be handsome in the usual way, she decided, but his rugged features suited her. His broad chest was covered with a thick mat of black hair that disappeared under the sheet. A thin, white scar trailed down his chest, half-hidden in the swirling hair. She couldn't resist the temptation to run her fingertip along the smooth line from the warm pulse in his throat to his navel. He stirred under her touch, and she shivered as pleasure tingled up her arm. The ache in her muscles took on a whole new meaning, and despite her killer headache, her body throbbed so sweetly. She stretched, wanting to purr like a contented cat. She waited for regret to flood her, but her satiated body wouldn't allow remorse to filter into her mind.

Was it so bad that they'd enjoyed each other? After all, it wasn't as if she didn't like Nick. She'd always thought he was sexy, even if she'd fought the attraction. And last night he'd proved what she'd suspected.

The faint wail of a siren roused her out of her doze. She opened her eyes to the sight of Nick, his face half-buried in his pillow. Well, the night might have ended, but the magic was still there. She leaned forward and kissed the soft skin in the hollow of his throat, savoring the salty-sweet taste.

Nick stirred under her touch, a faint smile crossing his lips. Leigh suddenly wanted him awake. She wanted to see his eyes darken with passion, feel his large, powerful hands stroking her. She kissed him again, this time on the mouth.

"Cara," Nick murmured, his arms tightening around her waist as his hands splayed on her naked back.

Leigh stiffened in surprise. *Cara?* Who the hell was Cara? His hands were moving, caressing her as she'd wanted, but now she had doubts. She'd made love to Nick, but had *he* been making love to her?

"Cara?" Nick was frowning in his sleep. "Cara, don't leave...."

A cold void formed inside Leigh. Oh, God. He'd used her as a substitute for another woman. Pain like she hadn't felt since her divorce ripped through her. She bit her lips to keep from crying out.

For four years, ever since the divorce, she'd avoided getting sexually involved with anyone. And now, in one night, she found herself falling for the same lure that had trapped her in a disastrous marriage. How could she have done it again? How could she have let sexual attraction sweep her into something like this?

Leigh lay still, afraid of awakening him, afraid to see the shocked recognition in his face. All she wanted now was to get away. She didn't want to hear the questions, the recriminations.

Tears slipped down her cheeks. A one-night stand. That's what she'd been, she thought. Anger built in her like a burgeoning volcano. Of course he'd been willing to accept her when she threw herself at him. Hadn't Maggie told her the punch was spiked? He'd been drunk!

Nick's arms relaxed around her, and Leigh slowly slid from the bed, keeping a wary watch on him. She shivered in the chilly room. With jerky movements, she gathered her scattered clothing and went into the bathroom, quietly closing the door behind her. Dropping her dress on the vanity, she turned on the water and surveyed her reflection in the mirror while waiting for the basin to fill. She even looked like a one-night stand, she thought grimly. Her brown hair was tousled; her mascara smeared. She washed and dressed with quick movements, promising herself a good, hot shower after she'd made her escape.

She tiptoed out into the main room and spotted her shoes under the chair next to the outside door. She froze in the middle of putting them on when Nick turned over in the bed with an unintelligible mutter. A beam of sunlight from a crack in the heavy drapes played across his long, lithe body outlined by the sheet pulled tightly around him. Leigh shuddered as a flash of desire crackled through her.

"You're a fool, my girl," she whispered. "Get out while the getting's good."

She grabbed her purse off the chair and, carefully opening the door, edged into the hall. She fled the silent hotel and dashed to her car, which was parked in the nearly empty lot. The sun, like a giant red ball, peeked through the low ground fog as Leigh aimed her car homeward. Guilt, anger and pain prodded her conscience like small devils with pitchforks. Leigh tried to put a clamp on her emotions, but no matter how hard she tried, she couldn't hide from the demons in her thoughts.

Leigh stood in the corner of the shower stall, letting the refreshing stream of hot water ease the tension in her body. After a thorough scrubbing, she finally felt as if she had cleansed all signs of the previous night from her skin, but she wished she could purge her memories. All too easily, images of Nick drifted through her mind. The sound of his laughter, the glow of passion in his eyes, and his hands... God, the memory of his long, strong fingers caressing, stroking her skin made her nipples tighten even more under the fiercely pounding water.

Leigh's breath caught in her throat. For crying out loud, she was doing it again! Getting herself all worked up over a phantom lover. Nick hadn't been making love to *her* last night. His tenderness and fire had been for some other woman, and she just happened to be in the right place at the wrong time.

But, still, a small voice in the back of her mind teased, what if he *had* been attracted to her a little, at least in the beginning? Leigh groaned and then frowned as she heard a sound. The phone?

She turned off the shower and opened the stall door. Yes, the phone. What if it was him? What would he say? What would *she* say? Relief swept through her as her answering machine intercepted the call and she heard Maggie's disembodied voice.

"Leigh? Are you there, Leigh? Pick up, please. I need to know you made it home okay."

Leigh slipped her full-length velour robe over her wet body, fumbling to fasten the zipper as she dashed to the phone before Maggie hung up.

"I guess you're not there," Maggie continued. "Lord, I hope you're all right. Call me—"

Leigh grabbed the receiver. "Maggie, I'm here. I was in the shower."

"Thank God. I was beginning to get worried when you didn't answer. Are you all right? I mean after last night..."

Guilt gnawed at Leigh's nerves. "Did you think I was that drunk?"

"Oh, honey," Maggie said with a chuckle. "You know me. No one has a simple illness—it's always life-threatening. I know I worry too much. Besides, it looked like Nick was taking good care of you."

Guilt turned to panic. "What do you mean?"

"Wh-why, nothing. I mean, well, it's just that the last time I saw you and Nick, you were dancing and..." Maggie sounded confused and Leigh's heart stilled in her chest. "Are you sure you're okay? You sound weird."

Leigh rubbed her hand across her aching eyes. "Yes, I'm fine. I just didn't get enough sleep." She hesitated, then rushed on. "I hope I didn't make a fool of myself last night."

Maggie's normal tones reassured her. "Don't be ridiculous. You were hardly roaring drunk, though you were obviously enjoying the party. Now, I'll hang up and let you get on with your day. Maybe by tomorrow you'll feel better."

Thank God for Maggie's uncomplicated nature, Leigh thought. Anyone else would have been asking a hundred questions, most of which she wouldn't have been able to answer.

"That's a good idea. I'm sure glad it's Sunday and I don't have to go to work."

"I'm with you. See you tomorrow. 'Bye."

Leigh placed the receiver in its cradle and headed for the kitchen. What she needed now was some coffee . . . and to make some hard decisions. She quickly brewed a pot and poured out a cup. Sipping at the dark liquid, she wandered back into her living room and seated herself on the wide sill of the bay window. She stared out at the quiet neighborhood.

So now what? What would she do if Nick decided last night was a signal for an affair? Would he become obnoxious? Somehow, Leigh couldn't picture Nick as the kind of boss who would start chasing his secretary around the desk. If worse came to worst, she could always quit. She knew she was good; she wouldn't have any trouble finding another job.

Leigh leaned her head against the wall. Who was she kidding? She would hate leaving Kiefer and Romano. To begin with, starting over would mean a cut in salary. She was too close to her goal to let that happen. Her law degree *had* to come first. She looked around the living room. Changing jobs would also mean a slowdown in the remodeling she was doing on her fix-it-up house.

Restless, she wandered around the living room. Be honest, Leigh, she told herself. She'd miss the excitement of working with Nick. She flinched from the thought. Only on a professional basis, she told herself fiercely. Besides, why should she leave? She hadn't been the one who had lured Nick up to that room.

At least, she didn't think she had.

Well, there wasn't any point worrying about it now, she decided. She would just wait until tomorrow and see what happened. After all, it would all depend on Nick's attitude.

Nodding with determination, Leigh set her empty cup on the coffee table and moved toward her bedroom. But a tiny doubt niggled at the back of her mind. Just *what* was Nick thinking now?

"'Bout time you made it in, boy!''

Nick groaned when he heard Drew's boisterous greeting Monday morning. He hated it when Drew put on his "good ol' boy" persona. For God's sake, the man graduated from Harvard summa cum laude. He was hardly fresh off the turnip truck.

"I'm not that late," he retorted.

"No, but this is the first time you've *ever* been late. Maybe we ought to put up a historical marker or something."

"Very funny," Nick said as he followed his partner through the busy reception area into Drew's office. He dropped into the client's chair. "Yesterday wasn't my best day."

Drew's expression sobered and he sat behind his massive oak desk. "Yeah, I found out this morning that Patterson loaded the punch with vodka."

"That idiot! He could have killed me!"

"You weren't drinking that much," Drew protested.

"No, no, but mixed with my allergy medicine . . ." Nick frowned. "No wonder I can't remember . . ."

"It's not a mistake he'll be making again soon."

Nick nodded and slouched further in the chair.

Drew eyed him closely. "At least you had fun Saturday night."

Nick looked at his partner, his eyes narrowed in thought. "I did? I only remember bits and pieces."

"Well, the last time I saw you, you were dancing with Leigh. And you seemed to be having a mighty fine time."

Nick pushed out of the chair and strode to the window. He stood, one hand in his pocket, staring at the late-morning traffic. He searched for memories of the party, but nothing came.

"Did she...did I...?" Nick's tie was suddenly too tight around his throat.

Drew looked bewildered, then comprehension dawned in his eyes. "You've got the hots for Leigh."

Nick couldn't answer. He felt as if he was back in high school, confessing all to his best buddy. Well, hadn't Drew been his friend since childhood? Nick wondered if his face was as red as it felt.

Drew slapped his knee as he laughed. "Nick Romano, crusader for the traditional family, wants to jump budding lawyer Leigh Townsend's bones?"

Nick glared at Drew. "Don't be crude. Leigh is a beautiful, intelligent, warm woman. She's sensitive and funny and... and..."

"And you've got the hots for her." Drew's expression held suppressed amusement.

His partner's smug demeanor melted Nick's embarrassment and he grinned. "Yes, I've got the hots for her. Satisfied?"

Drew grinned back and cocked his head. "So, how come you've never asked her out?"

Sorry he'd ever started this conversation, Nick threw himself back into the chair. "For crying out loud, she's my secretary!"

"So, were you planning to tell her that dating you is a condition of employment?"

"Of course not. But maybe it would make her uncomfortable turning me down."

"Leigh? I doubt it. She's the most up-front lady I've ever met." Drew rested his elbows on his desk, his hand rolling a pen along the surface. "How come you're just now getting interested in her? She's been working for you for over two years."

Nick shrugged. "I noticed her the first day, but at the time she was wary of men. I'm willing to bet she's been hurt badly by some guy."

"Her ex-husband?"

"Maybe. Whatever, it's only lately she has seemed more, er, accessible."

"So, now is the time for you to move in on her. You never know, maybe she's been secretly pining for you all this time."

Nick tossed him an exasperated glare, and Drew raised his hands in surrender. "All right, how 'bout this? Why don't you invite her to lunch? You know, in gratitude for all her good work. That will not only let you solve your puzzle, it will also give her a chance to know the real you, not the tyrant you are in the office."

"I'm not a tyrant!"

Drew cocked an eyebrow. "No? Then how come Leigh was your sixth secretary in ten months?"

"Because she was the only one who could spell," Nick mumbled. Drew never let him forget how he drove secretaries crazy, demanding perfection. Still, the lunch idea wasn't bad. Maybe if he took things slowly, gave Leigh the chance to know him . . .

He stood and strolled toward the door. "I better get to work. I'll think about your idea."

"Keep me informed," Drew teased as Nick left the office.

Nick strode into the small kitchenette that served as a break room. He poured himself a glass of cold tomato juice and leaned against the cabinet as he sipped it.

He tried to review his coming day, but thoughts of Leigh interfered. He couldn't even remember exactly when he had become aware of Leigh as a woman instead of just his secretary. Maybe it was the day she first wore that green dress he liked so much, the one with the short skirt that displayed those long, slender legs that drove him crazy. Or maybe it was the night they had worked overtime and she'd released her hair from her usual French braid, claiming it was giving her a headache. Oh, yes, his thoughts had definitely been unprofessional when he had seen those dark brown curls tumble around her shoulders.

Get honest, Nick, he told himself. He'd been aware of her from day one. She really hadn't been better than other secretaries when he first saw her. He'd simply been willing to wait until she learned to work with him. And now look at him. He couldn't give her a simple dictation without a glance from those gorgeous hazel eyes making him hard.

Saturday night he'd been ready to use the party as a means of making his move. Hell, he'd even made a good start, if his faulty memories were accurate. When had he stopped dancing with Leigh? Try as he might, all he could remember was something about a star that triggered confused feelings of satisfaction and need in him.

He sighed as he realized he was standing around wasting time. He rinsed out his glass, put it to drain and headed for his office. He hesitated outside the door, suddenly wary of what he would find. Would she smile at him with new awareness? He wished he could remember exactly what had happened. Well, there'd be no answer until he saw her. He opened the door and went through.

Leigh looked up from her work and smiled at him. "Good morning, Mr. Romano. You've only got forty-five minutes before you're due at the chamber of commerce meeting."

He smiled back and picked up a stack of papers on her desk. "I remember, Leigh." He watched her from the corner of his eye as he sorted through his messages. "The Christmas party was very nice, wasn't it?"

Her expression remained bland. "Yes, it was. Mr. Hutchinson called earlier. Would you like me to place a call to him?"

Nick nodded as he walked on into his office. He threw his mail on his desk and seated himself in his big leather chair. A twinge of disappointment niggled at the back of his mind. There was absolutely no change in her attitude. She obviously wasn't holding bad feelings about the party, but part of him was also discouraged that she didn't seem to be seeing him less as a boss and more as a man.

Okay, so she hadn't given him a big come-on. Wasn't that one of the things he prized in her? She was hardly likely to behave unprofessionally in the office.

Drew was right. He needed to give her a chance to get to know him outside the workplace. First chance he got, he'd invite her out to lunch. Yes, that felt right. Until then, well, he had work to do, and he'd better get to it.

He pulled some files toward him and flipped open the top one. An elusive memory flitted across his mind, the image of an angel in red. He grappled with the illusion. An angel in red? What did that mean?

Two

───

"Leigh, can you lay your hands on the Compton file?" Nick asked, standing in the door of his office.

Leigh lifted her fingers from the keyboard and looked at him, her brow knit in thought. "That industrial park deal you put together last year?" At his nod, she stood. "Yes, but it'll take me a minute."

As she moved around her desk, she jostled a container of pens and pencils, nearly upsetting them. She grabbed the holder before it fell, and Nick wondered why she flashed him such a guilty look. In fact, he thought, Leigh had been kind of antsy for the past couple of days.

"Sorry," she muttered as she walked to the file cabinet.

Nick leaned against the jamb and observed as she crouched to open the bottom drawer. Fascinated by the graceful movements of her slender hands, he watched her search for the file. So far he hadn't had much luck in getting closer to Leigh. Of course, it hadn't helped that he had spent so much time out of town on business, but still, not once in the past couple of months had she accepted a date with him. Oh, she'd always had a sound excuse. He certainly hadn't received an "I'm not interested" signal, but he couldn't say she had seemed attracted to him, either. He sighed and tugged at his tie until it loosened. So, why did he continue to hope?

His gaze skimmed over her as she flipped through the files. Because, he admitted wryly, he couldn't help himself. Something about her attracted him. It was more than her looks, though part of him had to admit he liked the way her straight heather wool skirt caressed her rounded bottom and displayed her long, slim legs. Maybe it was the fact she evaded him. Wasn't it said that elusive women brought out the hunter in men? He focused on her face and frowned.

"You look pale. Are you feeling okay?"

She gave him a guarded glance. "I'm just a little tired. I'm learning to clog and I think I overdid it last night."

"Clog? What the hell is that?"

She flashed him a weak grin and shifted her body before resuming her search.

"Clog dancing. It's an American folk dance. I had a class last night."

"Why?"

"Why?" Her expression was puzzled. "Why what?"

"Why are you taking clog dancing?" This was the first personal thing she had ever offered him, and he had no intention of losing a chance to open a communication line. "I mean, I never considered you as a folk dance kind of woman."

"Folk dancing is a hobby of mine, and it gives me an elective toward my degree," she said as she laid aside a file with a frown. "Looks like Connie's been in here again."

"How long have you been folk dancing?"

"I got interested in high school." She hesitated, her expression wary. "Why all the questions?"

He walked to the cabinet and braced his elbow on the top. "We've worked together for two years, and I don't really know much about you outside the office."

"Yes, well . . ."

"I think it's a shame when co-workers don't know much about each other, don't you, Leigh?" He liked the faint flush that swept over her cheeks. He couldn't recall ever seeing her so flustered, no matter what he'd thrown at her. Could it be she was more attracted to him than he thought? He hoped so.

"You know, I've never shown you how much I appreciate the fine work you do around here. How about if I take you to lunch today?"

"Ah, here it is." Her relief was patent as she lifted out the elusive dossier. She slammed the drawer and stood, holding it out to him.

"Thanks. Now about lunch..."

He noted her sudden pallor. He had only a glimpse of her wide, hazel eyes before her eyelids fluttered down and she quietly collapsed. Dropping the file, he caught her just before she hit the floor.

"Leigh?" Startled, he realized her skin was clammy, but at least she was still breathing.

He slid one arm around her shoulders and the other under her knees, lifted her and carried her into his office. Laying her gently on the sofa, he knelt on the floor. He took her hand and chafed the cold flesh, his thoughts frantic. He knew he should go for help, but the sight of her pale face, her limp body on the couch twisted his heart. He couldn't bear to leave her, even for a few minutes.

Come on, Romano, he told himself. *You learned first aid as a Boy Scout. Pull yourself together.*

He strode to his desk and, taking a small white plastic box from his bottom desk drawer, rummaged through it until he found what he wanted. Returning to Leigh, he sat beside her supine body and waved a broken ammonia ampule under her nose.

"Leigh? Come on, Leigh. Wake up."

She moaned and jerked her head away from the acrid odor. "Wha-a..."

Nick discarded the capsule and brushed a strand of hair off Leigh's cheek. An unexpected surge of protectiveness swept through him. Leigh had always been so competent, and somehow it didn't seem right she should now be help-less on his couch.

"How do you feel?" He braced his hand on the back of the sofa as she blinked, attempting to focus her gaze on his face.

"I . . . I'm fine," she said as she struggled to sit up.

"No, just lie there awhile. Give the blood time to get to your brain." He pressed her shoulders against the seat cushion, his thumbs caressing the satiny smooth skin of her throat. He almost groaned as he felt a sharp stab of desire.

She seemed mesmerized. He continued stroking her, fascinated to see tiny points of gold in her eyes that he had never noticed. He moved his hands until they cupped her face and he was close enough to feel her breath against his lips.

"I think it's there," she whispered.

"What?"

She grasped his wrists, tugging gently.

"I think I have enough blood in my brain now."

For a moment he couldn't understand what she was talking about, then he realized he had been within centi-meters of kissing her. Time seemed to expand before he could force himself to pull back. His gaze skimmed her face, and when he saw her blush, he smiled.

"Yes, your color does look better. Want to see if you can sit up now?"

Not waiting for an answer, he helped her swing her legs off the couch and stood waiting until she was sitting up-right. She started to rise, but he held up his hand.

"Wait a few minutes before you try to stand."

He returned to his desk and poured a glass of pale or-ange liquid from the thermal pitcher. Returning to her, he seated himself beside her and handed her the glass.

"Thanks," she murmured and took a sip. She grimaced and stared at the glass. "What is this?"

"Guava juice. It's full of vitamins," he said absently. "How are you feeling? Do you hurt anywhere?" He laid his hand on her forehead. "Maybe you have a fever."

She brushed away his hand. "Believe me, except for feeling a little shaky, I'm fine."

"Maybe you've picked up the flu bug that's been going around. I think you should go home for the rest of the day."

She gave him an exasperated glare. "For crying out loud, Mr. Romano, I had one of those flu shots you made the whole office take. I tell you, there's nothing wrong with me, and I'm not going home when we have so much work to do."

He gritted his teeth. Lord, the woman was stubborn. "Leigh, people don't just faint. There must be something wrong."

She jerked her head up, her eyes filled with startled horror.

"Leigh . . . ?"

He saw she had spilled her drink, and he whipped out a pale blue handkerchief from his inside jacket pocket. He dabbed at the sticky mess on her sweater. She gasped as his fingers brushed the soft curves of her breasts, and she snatched the handkerchief from him, her face scarlet.

"I'll do that!"

Nick hid a smile. This was turning into a farce. "At least you'll have to go home now. You certainly can't work in that condition."

She scowled at him. "I'll leave, but just long enough to change my clothes."

He lunged to his feet. "Oh, hell, Leigh . . ." One look at her face told him he wasn't going to get her to change her mind. "Fine. But I'll drive you."

"There's no need for you to do that. I can—"

"I'll drive you." He glowered at her, daring her to argue.

Suddenly she wilted against the back of the sofa and nodded her head, her eyes closed. "Okay. Thank you."

She looked so fragile, so tired, he wanted to hold her, protect her from whatever was worrying her. He instinctively knew she wasn't ready for him to be more than a boss yet. But he had every intention of using this opportunity to at least get her to see him as a friend.

"I'll get my car. And I'll send Maggie in to help you down to the main door."

She opened her eyes and gave him a wry smile. "What? You mean you're not going to carry me down to your white horse, Sir Galahad?"

He tilted his head and scanned her figure with blatant intent. "My car is eight blocks away, but I think I could make it," he teased. He reached for her, and she thrust out her hand with a gurgle of laughter.

"Never mind. I forgot you like to walk from your parking lot for exercise. I'd rather have Maggie's help. At least I won't have to worry about her dropping me."

He leaned over and brushed an errant curl behind her ear. "All right, give me twenty minutes, then come downstairs."

She watched him leave, her thoughts tumbling through her mind. She braced her elbows on her knees and buried her face in her hands. What was she going to do now? For over two months, she had carefully built defenses against the memories of the night of the Christmas party. Yet when she'd regained consciousness moments ago and seen the tender concern in Nick's eyes, those same memories came rushing in, flooding her with bittersweet pain. And right now she was even more vulnerable, especially if what she suspected was true. Never had she felt so alone.

"Leigh, what on earth happened?" Maggie sat down beside Leigh and pulled her against her ample chest. The scent of Maggie, so much like Leigh's mother, broke the tight feeling in Leigh's throat. Like a dam bursting inside her, tears poured down her face as huge sobs tore through her chest. She felt Maggie stroking her hair, crooning nonsense words in her ear. She didn't want this, but she couldn't seem to stop. Finally she felt the storm end and, embarrassed, she straightened, using Nick's stained handkerchief to wipe her face.

"Damn, now I have guava juice all over my face," Leigh said with an unsteady laugh. "And I probably look like a hag."

"No, no. You can hardly tell you've been crying." Maggie's worried gaze captured Leigh's. "Nick said you fainted. Are you okay?"

Leigh patted Maggie's hand. "I'm fine. I don't know why I fell apart like that. I must be more tired than I thought."

Maggie hesitated. "You know, Leigh, you've seemed worried the past few days. If you need someone to talk to, I'm always here for you."

Leigh looked at the older woman with affection. Dear Maggie. Ever since Leigh had joined the firm, a shy, inexperienced secretary in the typing pool, Maggie had tucked her firmly under her wing. Everything in Leigh wanted to lay all her problems on Maggie's capable shoulders, but how could she burden Maggie with what she feared? Especially now, when Maggie was so concerned about her husband being out of work.

"Hey, nothing's wrong. I guess I've been burning the candle at both ends, and it's finally caught up with me."

Maggie chuckled. "I'm not surprised. You have your college classes and weekends you're either scouring the flea markets or working on that house. And now clog dancing. Just talking about it makes me tired."

"Okay, so I'll give up the dancing..." Leigh said mockingly. "For now."

Maggie snorted. "Knowing you, you'll just start weight lifting or something. I don't know what to do with you. These past couple of months, you've kept yourself so busy. As if the devil himself were after you. Let me get your coat. Nick ought to be downstairs by now."

Maggie bustled into Leigh's office, and Leigh stood, breathing deeply to ease her light-headedness. *Maybe the devil is after me,* she thought as she left Nick's office. But if so, it was a devil of her own making.

* * *

Leigh unlocked her front door and stood just inside it until Nick walked past her. She took a quick look around the living room and sighed with relief. Thank goodness she had had time to do a fast pickup this morning before she'd left for work.

She stood watching as Nick openly investigated the area and wondered what he was thinking. The sun streaming in through the bay window made his hair shine blue-black, and she had an urge to see if it felt like the coarse silk she remembered. She let her gaze wander down his back, admiring how his muscular frame seemed to fit the large room. As he meandered around, she realized that, somehow, it was important he like her home.

After she'd bought the house, the living room had been the first area she'd worked on, and she was proud of how it had turned out. She'd replaced the wallpaper with oak paneling and thrown out a horrible carpet to make room for a thick-piled, sand-colored one. She'd picked out comfortable furniture and decorated the whole room in restful shades of brown, coral and turquoise. And now, with Nick there, for the first time she felt the room was complete. Which, she thought wryly, is crazy.

Nick halted beside the sawhorse next to the bookcase and glanced at her over his shoulder. "Interesting reading chair."

She laughed at his jest and tossed her purse on the small table next to the door. "I'm remodeling. You're likely to find stuff like that all over. You should have seen my bedroom before I finished it."

"Is that an invitation?"

Instantly his bantering question flooded her mind with hot, sweet images. Nick naked, his hair tousled, his heavy-lidded eyes simmering with passion against the tumbled sheets of her bed. She swallowed hard and forced her unruly thoughts into order. She couldn't afford such ideas, not today.

"No, that's not an invitation," she replied with a soft laugh. "But how about something to drink while you wait for me to change?"

She led him into the kitchen and smiled at his shocked expression. "As you can see, this is the room I'm working on now."

Used to the clutter, she'd forgotten the extra table where she'd piled her dishes until her cabinets were re-stained and re-hung. Boxes of floor tile lay stacked in the corner until she could get to them. She ignored the mess as she opened the refrigerator. "What will you have?"

"What have you got?" he asked, his warm breath stirring the curls around her ear.

Her mind went blank for a moment as she felt the touch of his body along her back when he peered over her shoulder. She gathered her thoughts.

"Uh, cola, iced tea, and...oh, there's some root beer, but it's been in there awhile, so it may be flat."

"Anything decaffeinated?"

Finding his closeness disturbing, she used the excuse of closing the door to gain some distance from him.

"No, but I have some orange juice if you don't mind frozen concentrate."

He stepped back and shrugged. "Don't go to any trouble. Water's fine."

"It's okay. Frankly, I'd like some juice myself, and it only takes a minute to fix."

She opened the freezer and withdrew the can. She could feel him watching her as she prepared the juice.

"Are TV dinners all you eat?"

"What?"

He nodded toward the refrigerator. "All you have in there are TV dinners. Is that all you eat?"

She suppressed a sigh. Honestly, sometimes the man was so irritating. "No, I'm the original junk-food queen. I usually just bring something home. The only time I eat the TV dinners is when I'm so involved in my remodeling, I don't have time to go out and get something."

"You know, junk food is very high in sodium and—"

"Yes, I know, Mr. Romano. We've all heard your views on junk food," she snapped as she poured the last can of water into the pitcher and stirred it with brisk strokes.

"How come you never call me Nick?"

Leigh's mind grappled with the change in subjects. "Well, it...it..." She took a deep breath to stop her stammering. "You're my boss. It wouldn't be proper to—"

"Come on, Leigh." He leaned against the counter, looking completely at home. "You sound like someone from the Dark Ages. You're the only one at the office who calls me Mr. Romano, and I've often wondered why."

Leigh knew why. It was one way she could keep herself distanced from him, but she couldn't tell him that, could she?

She averted her gaze and picked up her glass. "I don't know. I guess I just never thought of it."

"Good. Then you won't mind doing it, now that I've made you think of it, will you?" he asked with a laugh in his voice.

She couldn't tear her gaze from his face. This was the Nick she had seen at the party. Funny, warm and sexy. Her sensual awareness of him was so strong, she wondered why it didn't flash across to him like a lightning bolt, guaranteed to burn them both to a crisp. Time to get her crazy glands under control, she thought.

"All right...Nick."

His pleased expression caused butterflies to start quivering in her stomach, and she knew she had to have more space than the crowded kitchen allowed.

"I'd better change. Why don't you sit down and make yourself comfortable. I won't be long." She turned and headed for the living room, Nick right behind her.

Nick watched her walk down the short hall and go through a doorway before he resumed looking around the room. He liked what Leigh had done. The whole place looked restful, a room to sit in and enjoy a quiet evening after a long, busy day. He wandered over to the bookcase and scanned the titles. He noticed she had a wide taste in reading. He narrowed his eyes and peered closer. She even liked Agatha Christie, and he felt a surge of satisfaction. Good, they shared at least one common interest.

He sat on the three-piece sectional curved in front of the freestanding fireplace. He finished his juice and placed the empty glass on the coffee table. A familiar cardboard box caught his eye, and his breath caught as if he'd had a blow to the solar plexus. Slowly he picked up the container to examine it closer. Yes, it was the same thing he had seen at his sister's last week. For a moment, his brain spun as if out of gear.

"I'm ready if you are."

Leigh's voice startled him, and he rose, clutching the container. She buttoned the cuff on her long sleeve as she walked toward him.

She looked up from her task with a smile. "I tried to be as quick as I—" Her voice faltered when her gaze fell on the carton, and her face paled, then flushed. "Where did you get that?"

Embarrassment swept across her features and Nick clenched his jaw against the pain. Oh, God, don't let it be true.

He dropped the early-pregnancy test carton on the table. "It was just lying there. I didn't mean to snoop. Are you..." Having trouble getting the words out, he swallowed before trying again. "Are you pregnant, Leigh?"

"That's none of your damn business!"

"No? If you are pregnant, when will it become my business? When you're too big to fit behind your computer? When you call in sick from the maternity unit?" He sighed, then told himself to relax. "Leigh, I'd like to feel that I'm not only your boss, but a friend. If you could use a confidant, I'd be glad to listen."

Her trembling hand went to her throat, and she swayed as if she was going to faint again. Nick swiftly moved to her side and guided her to the sofa, seating her gently before sitting beside her.

"Talk to me, Leigh. Are you pregnant?"

"Yes...no...I don't know."

He could hear tears in her voice and placed his hand over hers as she twisted them together in her lap. He tried to come to grips with her answer, but all he felt was numb...and surprisingly, betrayed. No wonder she never accepted a date. She'd been involved with someone else. He closed his eyes against the surge of jealousy the thought gave him and ruthlessly blocked his anger. After all, she'd never belonged to him despite what he'd wanted.

"What do you mean, you don't know?" He forced his voice to remain calm.

She looked at him with overbright eyes. "The test came out positive, but the instructions said to go to a doctor to be sure."

"Have you?"

She shook her head. "I only took the test this morning."

"But it's possible?"

Her face flushed, and she averted her gaze as she nodded again. "I've been sick the past few mornings and I'm...I'm..."

"You're late."

The scarlet color in her cheeks deepened, and she tried to pull her hands from his.

"It's all right. Don't be embarrassed," he said tenderly as he tightened his grip. "I have four older sisters, all married, and usually one or the other is pregnant. That's how I recognized the box. My middle sister, Bella, has recently used one."

Leigh rose swiftly and walked to the bay window. "But she's married!"

"Are you going to be?"

She threw him a look full of despair before she bent her head and shook it. "I...I haven't seen him since the night we...we..."

The bastard, Nick thought with disgust. He had a pretty good idea what happened. Some Lothario had come up on her blind side, probably while she was still vulnerable from her folks' deaths. Nick was willing to bet Leigh had been much more serious than the man, and the jerk had hit the road. Leigh was the kind of woman who would equate making love with commitment. The creep probably took off as fast as he could. Well, the role of big brother wasn't what he'd envisioned with her, but if she needed a friend, he'd do his best.

"You know, most men will do the right thing if they know. Maybe if you told him—"

"No!" Leigh's tone was uncompromising, final.

"Leigh, you never know. Maybe he just panicked, and now he's ashamed to call you. It won't hurt to just talk to him."

"I can't. He . . . he has other obligations," she said in a rush.

"Oh, my God, you mean he's married?"

Leigh gave him a peculiar look and started to answer, then clamped her lips tight.

"With kids, too, I bet," Nick guessed.

Leigh shrugged, her gaze fastened on her feet.

Nick noticed how tired she appeared. He stood and went to put his arms around her. He tucked her head under his chin and reveled when she circled his waist with her arms and relaxed against him.

For a brief moment he imagined it was his baby she might be carrying under her heart, and the vision hit him with the impact of a pile driver. Thoughts of the coming changes in her body ran rampant in his mind. How her curves would become lush and full. The special glow her skin would radiate. The concept of how beautiful Leigh would become as her pregnancy advanced set his lower body throbbing. If it had been *his* child, then he would have been holding her with joy, with pride, and she would—

Halting his illusion, he reminded himself he was there as a friend.

"I think you have had about all you can take for right now. Why don't you change your mind and stay home for the rest of the day?"

She tensed in his arms, and the movement of her breasts against him sent a sharp bolt of need through him.

"Would you like me to resign my position, Mr. Romano?" she murmured, her face against his coat.

He forced his thoughts to remain brotherly as he pulled back far enough to see her worried eyes.

"Why would you leave?"

"Well, I'm going to be an unwed mother, and it could look bad for the firm."

He wanted to laugh at such absurdity, but she was so solemn.

"Nonsense. This is the nineties. Not many people mind that stuff anymore. And didn't we agree you were going to call me Nick?"

She rewarded him with a wobbly smile.

"You're not alone, Leigh." He smoothed the lines between her brows. "It would be wonderful for you and the baby if you didn't have to work, had someone to take care of you. As it is, you'll have to delay your plans to go to law school since—"

She jerked her face away from his hand and scowled. "No, nothing will stop me from becoming a lawyer."

"But, Leigh..." Nick noticed her pale face, her eyes faintly bruised. She was in no shape for an argument, he decided. He ran the back of his finger along the curve of her cheek. "What's important is you have friends, and we're all here for you. *I'm* here for you."

He gave her another quick hug, then firmly guided her to the sofa. "Now lie down. Take off your shoes and relax."

He slipped the shoes from her feet, took the afghan off the back of the couch and covered her.

"Give me your keys, and I'll see you get your car back. And don't worry about anything."

She searched the purse he'd retrieved and handed him the keys, holding them until his gaze met hers. "Thank you, Nick."

He smiled, his throat tight with all the unspoken words he wanted to say but knew she wasn't ready to hear. He bent and brushed a light kiss across her cheek.

"Rest. I'll see you tomorrow."

He walked quickly out of the house and got into his car. For a moment he sat, dazed, caught in a maelstrom of emotions. First came relief—Leigh was free, free of a creep who obviously didn't deserve her. He shouldn't feel glad about a situation causing her so much distress, but—

He slammed his fist against the steering wheel. *Yes,* he thought as hope surged in him. He still had a chance with her. He would comfort her, guard her, take such good care of her she couldn't help falling in love with him. Yes sir, he would become the best friend Leigh ever had.

Three

Three days later, Leigh hesitated outside her office and rubbed her damp palms against her coat. Nick would be in there, waiting to hear her news. She knew that, as surely as she knew her name. She wished she could call in sick, avoid facing him until she was used to the idea of being pregnant, but from now on she'd have to hoard her sick time. For a moment she struggled with the idea that she carried a new life inside her, but the concept was just too new. And now she had to face Nick. She closed her eyes, forced her anxiety to the back of her mind and opened the door. She stepped through the doorway of her office and smiled at the young, blond woman seated at her desk.

"Good morning, Connie. Sorry I'm late. Thanks for filling in. Ready to be relieved?"

"Oh, yes. And am I glad to see you." Connie stood, a pile of orange paper slips clutched in her hand. "All the stories I heard about him from the typing pool were true."

Leigh laughed as she tossed her purse on the surface of the desk and picked up the unsorted mail. "Nick's been an ogre today, has he?"

Connie rolled her eyes and grimaced. "Actually, he's only been here about ten minutes, but it's been the longest ten minutes of my life. He was unhappy you weren't here."

Leigh frowned. After the morning she'd already had, she didn't want to deal with an irate boss. "Didn't Maggie tell him—"

"Connie." Nick strode out of his office, his gaze fixed on a file in his hands. "Leigh isn't answering her phone at home, so I'm going over to check on her. Please cancel anything I've scheduled before lunch."

Connie fixed Leigh with a "See what I mean?" look. "She's here, Mr. Romano."

Nick looked up, and the anxiety in his eyes turned to relief. Leigh caught her breath at his expression. It had been so long since anyone had been concerned about her. Her heart seemed to stumble over its own beat. How could she feel pleased that Nick had been worried about her? The last thing she wanted was to get even more involved with him.

"Sorry I was late," she murmured as she gestured to the mail in her hands. "Just give me another moment and I'll bring in your correspondence."

Nick scowled and tossed his folder on her desk.

Connie took one look at him and thrust the stack of messages she held into Leigh's hands. "I'll get back to my own desk," she said as she scurried out of Leigh's office.

Leigh forced a laugh and looked at him with a mock severity. "Can't I be out of the office one morning without you terrorizing my replacement?"

"Where the hell have you been?"

His words flicked her like a whip and she stiffened. "I beg your pardon?"

"Didn't you think to let someone know you were going to be late?"

"I had a doctor's appointment. I—"

"You could have said something. It would be nice to know when my secretary is going to be late."

Leigh felt her temper start to shred and forced herself to place the mail with exaggerated care on her desk. "You were gone yesterday afternoon when my doctor's office called to say they could work me in early this morning. I told Maggie. Why didn't you ask her?"

"Maggie's not here. Her son had surgery last night—"

"Chris? What's wrong with him? What did Maggie say?"

"He had his appendix taken out, but evidently he's okay. In the future, I would appreciate it if you tell *me* when you're not going to be here."

Leigh gritted her teeth. So, his avowals of friendship were just a lot of hot air. Well that was all right with her. She preferred to keep things between them at a business level. "I apologize, sir. I assure you it won't happen again."

She noted with satisfaction that her formal attitude seemed to startle him. The anger faded from his expression and he extended his hand. "Leigh, I—"

"Will there be anything else, Mr. Romano?"

His mouth tightened and he glared at her. "No, Ms. Townsend. Do you suppose we could get some work done now?"

Leigh watched as he walked into his office and slammed his door. She jerked off her coat and hung it on the coat rack with a vicious wish that she was hanging one arrogant boss. She returned to her desk and reached for the mail, appalled to see her hands were trembling. *Damn the man!* She clenched her fists and took a deep breath. What she needed was a break. So what if she had just come in, she thought defiantly as she grabbed her cigarettes. If Nick didn't like it, he could lump it.

She stalked out of her office and caught sight of Maggie, leaning against the receptionist's desk, an amused smile on her face.

Leigh hugged her, then stepped back and examined the older woman's tired face. "You look beat. You must have had a rotten night."

"Are you kidding?" Maggie said with a laugh. "Chris survived the surgery better than I did. He's already being spoiled rotten by the nurses. But never mind about Chris. What I want to know is anyone bleeding?''

Leigh cast a guilty look around the main office. The rest of the staff was working, but she knew every ear in the place was alert, eager to hear everything. She grasped Maggie's arm and pulled her into the break room.

''I suppose we were heard all over the office,'' Leigh said ruefully.

''Just the thunder...not the words. That will make the grapevine happy. They can make the argument about any subject they want. What's he done now? I haven't seen you this peeved at him since your first month as his secretary.''

Leigh reached for her coffee mug. ''He's mad because I was late and he didn't get the message I'd left.''

''Oh, Leigh, that's my fault. When I called in, I forgot to say you would be late.''

Leigh poured a cup of coffee, picked out a chocolate-glazed doughnut from the box on the table and bit into it with relish. ''Don't worry about it. You had a lot on your mind.''

Maggie took a sip of coffee. ''Part of my worry was you. What about your appointment? There's nothing wrong, is there?''

Leigh hesitated, feeling a faint heat sweep over her face. Maggie had to know sometime; after all, in a few months everyone would know, especially if she remained at Kiefer and Romano.

''I'm pregnant,'' she answered, anxiously watching for her friend's response.

''I wondered when you were going to tell me.''

''You knew?''

''I suspected when you appeared so pale and tired all the time. The day you fainted confirmed it as far as I was concerned.'' She smiled with wry amusement. ''After all, I've been there six times myself.''

Her expression turned guarded and she gave Leigh a tentative smile. ''How do you feel about it?''

Leigh shrugged. ''At first, kind of scared. But now...I don't know. I wanted a baby so bad when I was married, but Brad wouldn't even talk about it. Of course, now I'm glad we didn't have children.''

''Your ex-husband was a jerk from what you've told me. So, do you want the baby?''

''Part of me does.'' She quirked up one corner of her mouth and Maggie smiled. ''But the rest of me is scared. I know it's hard to be a single mother.''

''Half the mothers in America are single and most of them are doing okay. You would, too. What about . . . ?'' She stopped, biting her lip.

''What about what, Maggie?''

''What about the father?''

Leigh felt her expression stiffen. ''What about him?''

''I know you haven't been dating. I mean, the only man you've been around for months is Nick and . . .''

Leigh jerked in her chair and the other woman's eyes widened. ''You mean . . . ?'' Maggie whispered.

Oh, Lord, Leigh thought. Trust Maggie to accidentally stumble on the truth.

''Nick?'' Maggie's expression was one of sheer shock, and she seemed unable to speak.

''Shh!'' Leigh clasped her hand over the older woman's gaping mouth. ''Do you want everyone in the office to hear you?''

Maggie pushed Leigh's hand away and glanced at the closed door. ''How could Nick be the father?'' she asked in a lower voice. ''Unless you two have been chasing each other around the desk, the only way you could be pregnant with his baby is by wishful thinking.''

''The Christmas party,'' Leigh mumbled. Avoiding Maggie's gaze, she lit a cigarette, then stared at it and groaned. ''I can't smoke now, can I? It's not good for the baby.''

She ground out the cigarette and Maggie patted her hand.

''Take up lollipops, it helps,'' she said in an abstract tone. ''You and Nick started dating back in December and you never said a word?''

Exasperated, Leigh let out a sharp breath. "We're not dating. We both had a little too much to drink and... and... well, it just sort of happened."

"At least Nick's not avoiding his responsibility."

"Nick doesn't know anything about it," Leigh said in fierce tones.

Maggie's eyes opened in astonishment. "Why not?"

"Because he doesn't remember."

"But, Leigh, you've got to tell him."

"No, and I don't want you telling him, either."

"But... but..."

Leigh took pity on her friend's confused state. "Trust me on this, Maggie. I have good, solid reasons for not telling Nick. I know he's an honorable man. Oh, he'd offer marriage, child support, all those kind of things, but don't you see? It would lead to all sorts of complications, and frankly I just don't want to deal with it all. It's going to be hard enough going through this alone without... without..."

"Leigh, you *have* to tell Nick. He has the right to know."

"Why?"

"Why?" Maggie sputtered. "He's the father!"

Leigh stared unseeing at the ashtray she twirled on the table top. "Maggie, I understand what you're saying, but I've been through this before. When I discovered Brad had been cheating on me, had never really loved me, it devastated me. It's taken me four years to regain my sense of self-worth, and I deserve better than a man who marries me because of a pregnancy."

Maggie's expression held understanding. "No one's saying you have to marry Nick. But you should tell him, if for no other reason than because your child is going to want to know someday."

Leigh chuckled without humor. "Can you see Nicholas Romano accepting anything less than full participation in raising his child? He'd never give me any peace. He'd badger me until I accepted his proposal out of sheer desperation to shut him up. No, I do this alone."

"But... but..."

"No, Maggie. I won't tell him. And if you do, I swear I'll quit and leave town if I have to."

Maggie remained silent, her face a mask of worry. Leigh silently begged her cooperation. She didn't want to face the thought of having to start over, but the vision of Nick knowing about his paternity gave her shudders.

Maggie nodded slowly. "All right. It's not my place to tell him, anyway. But in return I want a promise from you. Every child deserves to know, to receive as much as possible from each parent, even if they aren't together. So I want you to seriously reconsider telling Nick. It's only fair for all three of you."

Leigh slumped in her chair in relief. She couldn't see herself changing her mind, but she would admit the past few days had been too emotionally charged for her to trust all the decisions she'd made so far. Nick sometimes filled her thoughts to the exclusion of everything else.

Be honest, she told herself. It wasn't the thought of telling Nick about the baby that bothered her. It was the fact that he didn't remember. What had been so magical to her had evidently been just another encounter to him, easily forgotten. And if she did change her mind, did tell him, what good would it do? They were still miles apart in lifestyles.

She looked at her waiting friend. But Maggie was right. Nick did have a lot to offer as a father, even a single one. It was something to consider.

"Okay, I'll think about it."

The door opened and Nick came into the room, halting when he saw Leigh. She tensed, her mouth open for another bite of pastry.

"I didn't have breakfast," she said in gruff tones. "I'll work through lunch to make up the time."

Nick sighed. "Then you would be going without lunch. I don't mind you taking a break before you start work."

Leigh nodded, her throat too tight to speak.

Nick ran his hand through his hair. "Look, I'm sorry I came down so hard on you this morning. I was worried."

Again, Leigh could only nod.

He glanced at Maggie. "Would you mind if I had a few minutes alone with Leigh?"

"Uh, no," Maggie replied as she rose. "I have some papers I need to file before I go back to the hospital, anyway." She paused at the door and gave Leigh an encouraging nod toward Nick's back. "I'll leave you two to talk."

Leigh understood Maggie's silent message and frowned. "Don't worry about things here, Maggie. I'll take care of everything. Give my love to Chris."

"Sure." Maggie shrugged in resignation and left the room.

As soon as the door closed behind her, Nick sat across the table from Leigh. "What did the doctor say?"

Leigh darted a quick glance at him, and her heartbeat increased at the sight of him. He looked so concerned, so tender. She felt her irritation melt, change to a yearning she knew was dangerous. She looked down at her mug. "He said I was pregnant and that I'm basically healthy."

"That's good news." He hesitated and Leigh stiffened, afraid of what he might say. "Leigh, feel free to adjust your work schedule as you need to. I know there will be days when you won't feel like coming in or times when you will have doctor appointments. It might even be a good idea if you start training someone to take over for you occasionally, so they'll be ready when you take your maternity leave."

A warm, protected feeling flooded her. "I...I don't know what to say, Nick."

"Don't say anything. We have to take good care of you now."

Leigh scanned his features and wondered if her baby would look like his father. Would he have Nick's dark, thick hair, so like coarse silk? Or his deep brown eyes with those incredible long lashes? Even more important, would her son have Nick's intelligence, his determination, his sensitivity? Shocked, Leigh realized she was positive her child was a boy. Filled with secret laughter, she hoped the baby wouldn't share Nick's love for bean sprouts.

Staring at him, Leigh visualized Nick as a father. She could see his strong hands holding a small boy on his shoulder as they watched a parade. And she could hear his patient voice as he taught his son how to fish. Would it be so terrible if she told him the truth about the baby?

"Nick..."

"I don't want you to worry about anything, Leigh. If the baby's father can't do the right thing, I will."

His eyes glazed over slightly as if he viewed something deep inside himself. "There was a time when I could... when I thought..."

He shook his head, as if to chase off a bitter memory, and grinned. "Anyway, I think I would make a great surrogate father."

Leigh's throat tightened. How could she have forgotten Nick was a haunted man? "I'm sure you would, Nick." The words sounded forced to her own ears.

"Well, I didn't mean to get gloomy." He stood, then hesitated. "I'll be in Drew's office. When you get back to your desk, will you please type up the notes I left?"

Leigh sighed in relief. "Yes."

He turned and headed out of the room, pausing at the door to look at her over his shoulder. "I have some yogurt in the refrigerator, Leigh. Feel free to help yourself. You need to start eating better, especially now."

He left and she closed her eyes in despair. Oh, Lord, how did he do this to her? She felt as if she was on a seesaw. Every time she set her boundaries, Nick's tender concern made her doubt her decisions. She couldn't let him get too close. She *wouldn't* let him get too close. All she had to do was be firm.

Leigh returned to her desk, but found herself staring at Nick's empty chair through the open door of his office. She had no trouble putting an image of Nick in the chair. Decisive, confident and, since the morning he drove her home, considerate. And don't forget sexy, a small voice in her mind told her. Suddenly the image she saw behind Nick's desk was naked, wearing only the same wicked smile he had the night of the Christmas party. She groaned and buried her face in her hands. Something told her she had opened Pandora's box and who knew what would come flying out?

Leigh steered her car up the slight slope of her driveway and parked. After turning off the ignition, she leaned her head against the headrest and sighed. A pleasant lassitude made her reluctant to leave the warm car for the cold twilight. She always enjoyed her infrequent after-work swims, but sometimes it eased her tension too well. There was little chance she would get much done at home tonight, especially after the emotionally fraught day she'd had.

An indistinct movement caught her attention from the corner of her eye, and she jerked her head toward the door. Oh, Lord, there was someone on the porch and the damn light was burned out. For a moment fear tightened her throat and she hastened to assure herself that the car door was still locked. Then she recognized Nick walking down the steps.

She tugged on the handle, swinging the door wide. "You scared the hell out of me. What are you doing here?"

Nick took her battered gym bag from her as she scooted out of the car. "I came bearing gifts. You should leave a light on when you know you'll be coming home late at night."

"Did you come all this way just to check out my security?" she muttered. She fumbled in the shadows, attempting to find the unseen keyhole.

She felt more than saw his grin. "Hardly. I brought dinner. Let's get in. It's freezing out here."

Leigh held the door open to let him pass. "Why didn't you wait in your car?"

"I had to park halfway down the street."

As Leigh closed the door, she noticed all the cars parked along the curb. Her neighbor was probably having one of her interminable parties. At least, she thought gratefully, the bitter wind meant no open windows and that meant no raucous music.

She slipped off her coat and followed Nick into the kitchen. She noticed the flat, wide box he set on the counter before he turned and placed a carton of milk in the refrigerator.

She lifted an eyebrow at him. "Pizza? I think the cold has frozen your brain. I can't believe you actually walked into a pizzeria to order America's favorite junk food."

Nick laughed as he opened the carton. "A veggie pizza." He snagged two plates from a pile stacked on the crowded extra table. "It's the closest I could come to a good compromise for both of us."

Amused, she crossed her arms and leaned against the counter. She watched as he laid two sections on each plate, then slid them into the microwave. "And the milk?"

"I noticed you didn't have any the other day, so I brought some with me."

"I don't keep milk because I don't drink it."

"But you haven't been pregnant before. Milk is good for the baby."

Her breath caught in her throat. She wished she could be as casual about her pregnancy as he was. But of course, unlike her, he wasn't hiding anything.

"Got any napkins?" he asked as he set silverware and glasses on the table.

She shook herself free from her uncomfortable thoughts and moved to the holder over the sink. "I'm out. I've been using paper towels."

The microwave beeped and Nick pulled the plates from the oven. "Dinner is served."

"Take the pizza into the living room and I'll bring the drinks." Leigh saw his quizzical expression and resigned herself to her fate. "Yes, I'll bring the milk."

He smiled but left the room without saying anything. She poured two tall glasses with the cold liquid and followed him through the doorway.

Nick stood beside her entertainment center, flipping through her collection of compact discs. He looked up as she entered.

"Do you have anything besides country?"

She grinned at him and set the glasses on the coffee table. "You and my mother." She moved next to him and pulled an unopened Glenn Miller disc from behind the storage rack. "She hated country, too. She spent her entire marriage trying to get my father to listen to something else, anything else."

Nick placed the disc in the player and closed it. "Did she succeed?"

"Nope." She sat on the sectional, watching him adjust the volume. "She sent that to me, hoping she'd do better with me."

Leigh noticed he had closed the front drapes and lighted the thick, peach candles on the coffee table. Their fragrant scent competed with that of the pizza, and Leigh picked up a hot slice, gingerly handling it. She took a bite, savoring the rich tomato sauce and stringy cheese. She saw Nick watching her, a slight smile on his face.

"Well?"

"Not bad. Of course, it would taste better smothered with sausage and pepperoni," she said with mock solemnity.

Again he laughed and she let the sound flow over her like warm honey.

He bit into his own pizza, and Leigh found herself fascinated at the sight of his tongue sweeping along his bottom lip, capturing a stray morsel of green pepper. She shivered at the thought of his tongue on her lips. Attempting to distract herself, she concentrated on her food.

"What kind of music do you usually listen to?" she asked.

"Some classical, big band, but mostly jazz."

"Jazz?"

"Why are you so surprised? A lot of people like jazz."

"Yes, but...well, jazz seems a little...er, wild for you."

He glanced at her, a faint smile on his lips. "Just exactly how do you see me, Leigh?"

She thought for a minute. "Conservative, organized . . . I don't know. Kind of . . ."

"Stuffy?"

She shrugged helplessly. "I only see you in the office."

"Well, I'll have you know I don't live behind a desk. I jog five miles a day. I like science fiction movies and Agatha Christie mysteries. I've even been known to go completely crazy and attend the stock car races."

"I love stock car races, but I haven't gone for years. No one else I know likes them, and I hate to go alone."

"We'll have to plan on going when the season opens. Do you want any more pizza?"

Leigh stared at her plate, surprised to find she had eaten all her pizza. "No, those slices were extra large. I'm full."

"That's why I always buy at Gino's. That way I have some left over for breakfast."

She burst out laughing. "Nick Romano eating cold pizza for breakfast? The mind boggles. No," she said as he reached for the dirty dishes. "Since you cooked, I'll clean up and get some coffee."

"None for me, thanks."

"It's decaffeinated." At his surprised look, she scowled. "Okay, okay. So I switched when I suspected I was pregnant. Don't make a big deal out of it."

"Who, me?"

She laughed and went into the kitchen, carefully balancing the dishes. She started the coffeemaker, then loaded the dishwasher. Tension began to build in her as she considered what would happen now. Why had Nick come? What was on his mind?

She poured out two mugs of coffee, and grabbing them, walked back into the living room.

Nick was back at the CD player. "I thought I could at least let you have your kind of music part of the evening," he said as he started a country disc.

She set the mugs down and curled up in the corner of the sectional. "Thanks."

Nick settled next to her, close enough to start her skin tingling, but not touching her. Leigh felt vaguely disappointed. Not wanting to admit the possible reason for her disappointment, she wiggled around until she was facing him with a more comfortable distance between them.

"Okay, you've wined and dined me, so to speak," she said, cradling her mug between both hands. "Why do I get the impression there's a reason for your generosity?"

Nick stared at his cup, then directly at her.

"I got to thinking about this morning and felt I owed you an explanation."

"About why you overreacted?"

He grimaced. "Yes, only I'm sure you're not going to like it."

"Try me."

"Somehow, I got the idea you were late because you were getting an abortion."

"*What?*" Leigh jerked upright, almost spilling her coffee. "Are you crazy? Whatever made you think I would do such a thing?"

He waved his hand in a calming gesture. "I know...I know it's crazy. But...." He hesitated, then continued. "You see, there was this girl...in college. She and I...well, we lived together. Oh, we used all the trendy arguments. Our love didn't need the shackles of a marriage license, the outdated restraints of our parents' generation." He looked at her. "You know what I mean?"

Leigh nodded, her throat dry and tight. She didn't want to hear this, but couldn't force herself to stop him. She *had* to know. Was she going to hear about the mysterious Cara?

He relaxed slightly, his expression relieved. "Anyway, she got pregnant, and when she told me, I figured we'd get married. I'd get a job, go to night school while she took care of the house and the baby. It seemed the right thing to do." He fell silent, lost in his thoughts.

Leigh cleared her throat, fighting to get the words out. "What happened?"

"I didn't see her for a week. When I called her house, all her dad would say was she was sick and to stay away from her. Finally he told me she had had an abortion and that she wanted to finish college, not get married. Just before he hung up, he told me to stay the hell out of her life."

Leigh gasped as a cold pain raced through her. She could only imagine the kind of anguish Nick must have gone through. She laid her hand over his, squeezing gently. "Oh, Nick. I'm so sorry."

He turned his hand, interlocking his fingers with hers. "It's okay, Leigh. It hurt at the time, but I've come to terms with it."

She couldn't help herself; she had to ask. "Did...did you love her?"

"I thought I did. I was young and brash, thought I had the world in the palm of my hand."

"Do you still see her?"

"No." He bent his head, seeming to examine her hand as his thumb stroked lightly along the back of it, sending streamers of fire up her arm. "In a way Darlene was right. We weren't ready to get married."

Darlene? Confusion jumbled in Leigh. This wasn't the woman haunting Nick, the one named Cara. She wondered how many women he had haunting him. She immediately felt guilty for her thoughts. Nick had just revealed an unhappy part of his past and all she could do was speculate on the other women in his life.

"You didn't have any control over what happened. Darlene made the decision, right or wrong, and you had to go on from there."

He scowled. "Yes, it was her decision, but she shouldn't have taken that step without even discussing it with me. And it made me understand that living together was a cop-out. If you care enough about someone to live with them, you marry them."

He looked at her, a rueful smile on his face. "Then, when you told me you were going to take care of your pregnancy, you see why..."

"Why you thought I might do the same thing."

He shrugged and looked straight at her. "I guess so."

"Nick, I'm not some teenybopper, unable to support and care for a child. As long as I can remember, I've wanted to be a mother and, if I keep it, I plan to take good care of this baby."

"What do you mean, if you keep it?"

"I'm thinking about giving the baby up for adoption." Startled at the pained expression on Nick's face, she laid her hand on his and flinched as he gripped. her fingers. "There are hundreds of willing couples, eager to adopt, who could provide the baby with a stable, two-parent family."

"No! You can't do that."

Leigh watched in amazement as Nick stood and paced rapidly in front of the sofa. "How could you just give away your child? Never know where he is or if he's okay. Never know if—"

"Nick." Leigh extended her hand, halting him mid-stride. "It is only one option that I'm considering. I owe it to the baby to make the best decision I can, but I haven't made up my mind yet."

Nick returned to his seat, visibly restraining himself. "Good, you think about it. But I'm willing to bet you'll find you're not the kind of woman who can give away her baby. Family means too much to you."

"Nick, I have no family. There'd be just me and the baby."

He picked up her hand where it lay in her lap. "But you have me, and you'll let me help, won't you?"

Uh-oh, Leigh thought. *That isn't a good idea.* "I appreciate the offer, but I don't want to impose on you."

"What are you going to do when you need something heavy moved during your renovation? Or you're too tired to go grocery shopping?"

She hated it when he smiled like that. It made him so damned irresistible. "I'm sure Maggie and her husband will be glad to help me."

"But they live in the next county. I live only ten minutes away."

"Yes, but..." Panic surged in Leigh. How could she get out of this gracefully? She couldn't let him get involved in her life and with her pregnancy. How would she ever keep the truth from him?

"I would drive you crazy. I mean, I throw up a lot and . . . and I cry all the time and . . ." Leigh knew she was babbling.

Nick chuckled. "I know. I'm experienced at all the idio-syncrasies of pregnant women."

Confused, Leigh could only look at him.

"My sisters. I saw it all with them. It won't be so hard, Leigh. Any time you need something, you just give me a call."

And how often she called, Leigh thought, would depend on her. It wouldn't be as if he were living with her, under-foot all the time. She would just make sure she never needed to call him.

"Well, if you're sure," she said slowly, uncertainly.

"Great." Nick leaned forward and brushed his lips across her cheek. He walked to the chair where he'd thrown his coat and picked it up. "Now, I'll be going so you can relax before you go to bed."

Relax? With the spicy scent of him filling her head? With her skin tingling from his kiss? Not in a million years. She joined him by the door.

"Do you know that eating a couple of dry crackers when you first wake up, before you try to get out of bed helps with the nausea?" he asked as he buttoned his coat.

Leigh nodded. "Yes, the doctor told me. Nick, thanks for the pizza. And . . . and for being there for me."

His large, tender hands cupped her face as his gaze ex-amined her features. Beguiled, she wanted him to kiss her, really kiss her. She wanted to explore the dark mystery of his mouth. She leaned toward him, her hands gripping his elbows for support.

"You know, in that red dress, you look like a naughty angel," he murmured, his breath warm against her lips.

She pulled away from him. What made him use those words, almost identical to the ones he used at the party? Was he starting to remember? She felt her eyes widen in dismay.

"Strange," he said, frowning. "Do you feel it, too? That sense of déjà vu? Maybe we knew each other in another lifetime," he joked.

She couldn't have answered him if her life depended on it. He flashed her a smile and opened the door.

"Good night, Leigh. See you tomorrow."

She stood in the open doorway and watched him stride through the dark. Long after he disappeared from sight, she remained locked in place until the cold forced her inside. Even in the warmth and light, she was unable to dispel the heaviness in her heart. What if he remembered? She shivered and knew it wasn't just the cold that caused the tremors. If Nick ever found out about the baby, there'd be hell to pay. And she hoped she'd have the price.

Four

―――

"Where's the man when I need him?" Leigh muttered. She kicked the bottom of the door with the flat of her foot. The door didn't budge, just as it hadn't budged the last time she'd kicked it. In fact, the damn thing hadn't moved since it had swung shut, trapping her inside the empty closet. Leigh sighed and relaxed against the back wall, her arms draped loosely over her bent knees.

Two weeks ago she'd told Nick she'd call him if she needed him. Of course she'd planned on never calling him, and she hadn't, she thought with pride. Not that it had made any difference. In fact, she'd spent more time with Nick than she would have if they'd been Siamese twins.

If he wasn't at the house with something he was sure she needed, he was calling her. Last Sunday, he'd phoned her three times and still managed to be there for dinner that night. He brought her packed lunches at work and took her grocery shopping.

And the lectures, she sighed as she halfheartedly kicked the door again. Dear Lord, she now knew more about nu-

trition than a licensed dietician. Nick was dragging her to
a healthier life-style, kicking and screaming every inch of
the way. She smiled. On the other hand, it *was* kind of nice
being pampered this way. Now, if she could only get out of
this damn closet.

She rose carefully, so she wouldn't bang her head on the
clothes bar, and checked the door again, determined to find
some way of forcing it open. In the dark she could feel the
irregular edges she hadn't noticed in the light. It wasn't any
wonder the door had jammed so tightly. "Why couldn't it
have done this while I was on the outside?" she muttered,
pounding the door with her fist.

She slid down to the floor, hitting her empty mug with
her shoe, sending the cup rattling against the wall. What she
wouldn't give for another cup of coffee . . . and a cigarette.
Drawing her legs up, she buried her face against her bent
knees. God, a person who was giving up smoking shouldn't
go through this kind of ordeal, she mused. They should
have butterflies and rainbows and—

"Leigh?"

She jerked up her head. "Nick!" she called as she
jumped to her feet. A sharp pain radiated from the top of
her head, and her eyes watered. "Oww! Damn it!"

"Where are you?"

She rubbed the sore spot on her scalp as she grabbed the
doorknob. "Here. In the back bedroom. Get me out of
here."

She heard footsteps outside the door. "Where?"

"In the closet."

She felt him tugging at the door. "Boy, it's really stuck."

"Did you think I was in here because I couldn't find my
way through the dark?"

His chuckle increased her irritation. "You want a cigarette, don't you?"

"How can you tell?"

"You always get sarcastic when you crave one."

"Well, don't worry. I didn't bring any with me, though
I might have if I'd known I was going to be locked in a
closet for hours."

"No, you wouldn't have. You've been doing a great job of quitting and I'm proud of you."

"Thank you." His praise mollified her.

"How long have you been in there?"

"Since about six. I thought I'd get a head start on the remodeling before you got here." She heard a faint whispering sound on the door. "What are you doing?"

"Just checking the door. I'll have to pry it off. It's too badly distorted to use, anyway. Stay right there. I'll be back."

"Is that supposed to be a joke, Romano?"

There was no answer and she tilted her head, trying to hear. "Nick?" She realized he had left. "Great. Just leave me here."

She slumped against the door. Time seemed to crawl by. Darn it, where was he? She thumped the door with her fist. "Nick?"

She listened carefully, but couldn't hear anything. She slid down the door. He probably went for help, she decided. But how long does that take?

"That's right, Nick. So what if I starve to death? Just leave me to the creepy crawlies to—"

"What are you raving about?"

His sudden question combined with a loud metallic thud caused her to jump.

"Where have you been?"

"I've only been gone for a few minutes." His voice was muffled by a metallic jangle.

"What are you doing?"

"I'm good, Leigh, but I can't rip a door off with my bare hands. I went downstairs to get your toolbox. Now, stand away from the door in case splinters go flying.

She sat with her back to the door, facing the rear wall. "How did you get in?"

"When you didn't answer my knock, I broke the window in the kitchen door and let myself in."

A loud screech startled Leigh and it took a minute before she understood. Nick was removing the hinge pins.

"You broke my window?"

The sound of the second pin being withdrawn made Leigh's teeth hurt.

"Honestly, Nick..."

"For Pete's sake, Leigh. You've already fainted once. What was...I supposed...to think when...your car is in...the drive and you don't...answer the door?" His words were interspersed with grunts. "There," he said with satisfaction as she heard the door crack.

She whirled around and saw he had opened a small space along the length of the door. He peeked in the aperture, a crowbar in his hands. "Just a moment and I'll have this big enough you can slide out."

He dropped the tool and, bracing his back on the jamb, pushed the door wider. It was slow work, forcing the warped door to open, and Leigh enjoyed every second. The sight of his flexed muscles under his form-fitting T-shirt made her mouth water. What she wouldn't give to have those arms around her. She would dance her fingers up those hard bulges, then down to another hard—

"Leigh? Don't you think it's wide enough to get through?"

Nick's voice cut through her fantasy and she gulped. He was watching her, his expression puzzled. Lord, she had to stop these wild daydreams.

"Ah...I've been in the dark too long. I couldn't see for a moment."

"Right."

She saw his smug smile and knew he was aware she had been admiring his build. She frowned as she turned sideways and scooted out of the closet. She glanced at the broken door.

"This is terrific. Not only do I have a broken window to get fixed, but a door to replace, too," she said crossly.

Nick laughed. "So much for gratitude."

She instantly felt ashamed. It wasn't Nick's fault that she found him so attractive she couldn't keep her eyes off him. "I'm sorry. I guess being shut up so long made me grouchy. Thanks for getting me out, Nick."

He stepped closer and brushed a stray curl off her cheek. "If you're really grateful, I can think of a better way to say thank you."

Enthralled, she gazed into his eyes and vaguely noticed their color was a rich, dark chocolate, reminding her of her favorite food. His warm breath drifted across her cheek and his spicy male scent made her think of warm midnight breezes on her naked body.

"What way?" she whispered through a dry throat.

"Breakfast," he whispered back.

"Breakfast?" She blinked to break the spell of his gaze and stepped back. "Oh, yes. Breakfast. Sure, why not?"

Leigh walked out of the room, fully conscious of the man following her with the toolbox. She hadn't missed the way his faded, worn jeans molded over his hips and tapered down his muscular legs. She wished, manners be damned, he was in front of her so she could watch his gorgeous backside. Inwardly she groaned. For crying out loud, it was only eight-thirty in the morning. If she didn't get her rambunctious notions under control, she'd jump his bones before lunch.

"How about cereal and toast?" she asked as she opened the refrigerator. "And I've even got bananas to put on top of the cornflakes."

"A hot breakfast would be better. How about omelets?" He poured two cups of coffee and handed her one. "The weatherman says a cold front is coming in. We might even get sleet."

"Oh, I don't feel like messing up the kitchen." She avoided his eyes as she dug out bowls. *Please, Nick, don't push it,* she silently pleaded.

"Okay. Why don't you make some oatmeal and I'll handle the toaster." He gave her a coaxing smile, a stray lock of hair curled over his forehead. "I'll make cinnamon toast."

Darn, now I'll have to tell you, she concluded. She took a deep breath. "I don't cook."

His eyes widened slightly. "Why not?"

"Because I can't. In fact, I hate it. If I don't burn everything, then it's underdone." She felt like a fool and resented it. So what if she couldn't cook? She had other talents, didn't she? "My mom tried to teach me, but I preferred to help my dad out on the farm than spend time in the kitchen." She gave him a mocking grin. "Unless you plan on putting up wallpaper with the leftovers, I wouldn't let me make oatmeal.

He grinned back at her. "Okay, I'll make the oatmeal. You do the toast, and be generous with the cinnamon." He arched his eyebrow. "You can manage a toaster, can't you?"

"Sometimes." She chuckled. "If I make the first two slices a sacrifice to the gods of kitchen appliances."

He laughed and she loved the way the sound rumbled out of his broad chest. She slid two pieces of bread into her toaster, then stood leaning against the counter, content to watch him hustle around the room.

"If you don't cook, are you still eating out all the time?" he asked as he carefully measured out water and put it to boil.

"Sure."

He looked up at her, his expression serious. "That's not good. Not only is fast food less nutritious, but it's so expensive. You know, when the baby comes, you're going to have a lot of costs."

Leigh scowled. The baby again. Did the man never stop? Her pregnancy occupied most of her thoughts, too, but he had worrying down to an art form.

"Fast foods aren't so bad nowadays," she replied with a grin. "Most of them offer healthy menus, even salad bars."

"What about the baby? Are you going to take him out to eat all the time?"

Leigh bit the inside of her cheek, reminding herself he was just trying to help. *Don't lose your temper, Leigh. Keep things light.*

He stirred the oats into the boiling water and turned the heat down. He scowled as he sprinkled raisins into the simmering cereal. He looked up at her, his expression lighting with a smile. "I have it. We'll get you a house-keeper. She can do the cooking and the heavy cleaning."

Leigh saw red. "Thank you very much," she said in crisp tones. "But I don't need a housekeeper. She would cost more than eating out all the time. Besides, I can take care of myself."

"When you're not getting yourself shut up in closets."

"You . . . you . . ."

"Now, don't get huffy, Leigh. Didn't I promise I would help you with this baby?"

"Help?" she said through gritted teeth. "Help? You aren't helping. You're taking over my life!"

"I think you're exaggerating a—"

"You think so? Come with me." She grabbed his hand and pulled him to the walk-in pantry. "Look at this," she said as she waved her hand at the crowded shelves. "This is all the food you have brought over in the past two weeks. I don't even know what half this stuff is."

"I may have gone a little overboard, but—"

"Oh, really? Let's see what else we can find, shall we?"

Ruthlessly she stalked into the living room, tugging him along. "What's wrong with this picture?"

As he looked around, she focused her gaze directly on the problem. She pointed to the overflowing bookcase. "There. It looks like the maternity care annex of the library. If you bring me one more book, I'll have to start cataloging them. I can't believe how many books there are about prenatal care and you seem to be bound and determined I have every one of them, aren't you?"

He shrugged his shoulders and jammed his hands into his pockets. "Well, I just thought you would like to know everything you could about what's happening to your body."

"I know what's happening to my body—I'm having a baby. The operative word is *I*."

"Leigh, this can't be good for the baby." He reached for her and she stepped back.

Tears stung the back of her throat. The baby. Always the baby. What about her? For two weeks he had treated her just like another pregnant sister. How could she be attracted to a man who obviously considered her as sexy as a brood mare?

"I'm concerned about my pregnancy, but you're obsessed with my baby. I feel like a damn incubator." Her anger blazed like a cold blue flame through her heart. She stalked him, jabbing her forefinger into his chest to emphasize her words. "I don't know why you're doing this. Pity, an overwhelming need to control, or maybe you're looking for a replacement for the child you lost. But I do know I've had as much as I can take."

With each poke of her finger, he backed away from her until she had him against the front door.

"Leigh, I'm sorry—"

"I don't care," she snapped. She grabbed his coat off the doorknob, threw it at him and, pushing him out of the way, opened the door. "Go home, Nick. I've had all your nagging I can take today."

"Leigh, I understand you're moody. The baby has put your hormones out of whack."

He said *that* word again, she thought, enraged. *Baby.* She blew up like a volcano. "Stop it!" she screamed.

The sound of her cry doused her fury, and she wasn't sure who was more startled, she or Nick. She understood the bewilderment in his expression; she felt confused herself. Was it his fault he'd involved himself so thoroughly in her pregnancy? What happened to her promise to herself that she wouldn't let him get too close? The first time he showed up with that sack of books, she should have sent him on his way. Well, it wasn't too late, she decided.

"Nick, I'm sorry I yelled like a fishwife. You're probably right about my hormones. I do seem to be a little impatient lately, but to be honest, you're driving me crazy. I promised you I would phone if I needed anything, and I will. However, until you can start treating me like you used to, I think we need to spend less time together. Please, go home."

"But I thought we were going to rebuild the back bedroom. You'll need—"

"No, I don't *need* anything right now. I've lost my eagerness to work today." She pushed him out of the doorway, ignoring the distressed expression on his face. "Starting now, I'd rather you didn't come around unless I invite you. I'm sure your sisters find your knowledgeable support a comfort, and if I find I need someone, you'll be the first person I'll call. Otherwise, I'll see you in the office Monday."

He opened his mouth to answer as she gently shut the door. She leaned against the door and closed her eyes. She willed him to leave without further protest, and after what seemed an eternity, she heard him leave the porch. The sound of his car driving away filled her with forlorn satisfaction. She had gotten what she wanted, hadn't she?

The piercing shrill of her smoke alarm jarred her and she dashed to the kitchen. Smoke poured from her toaster. She yanked the lever, and two blackened chunks of bread popped up. She threw them into the sink, swearing under her breath at the heat stinging her fingers. She turned off the flame under the oatmeal and then opened the window to clear the smoke.

She looked at the disaster area her kitchen had become. The smell of scorched oatmeal competed with the stench of burned toast. Cold air swept in from the opened window as well as the broken one, sending goosebumps up her arm. She laughed without humor. The kitchen gods were certainly getting their revenge today. Unwilling to wait until the kitchen was clear of smoke, she stood on a chair and removed the batteries from the alarm.

She hopped down and, retrieving the oatmeal pan, started scraping the lumpy mess into the garbage disposal.

Already she missed him. She realized she'd had hopes, dreams of Nick being as crazy about her as she was about him. But reality is a cold mistress, she decided. What man would fall in love with a woman he thinks is carrying another man's child? Especially a man still mourning a lost love. And did she really want another serious relationship now? What about her plans, her goals?

A movement caught her attention and she looked at the back door. She saw a man's white handkerchief tied to a long, slim branch extended through the broken window. She rose and saw Nick, one hand raised in the peace sign while the other waved his makeshift truce flag.

"Pax?"

She felt her heart stop momentarily, then resume its beat with a heavy pounding. With ruthless calm, she forced down the anticipation rising in her. "I don't believe I called for help."

"I remembered the broken window. Since I broke it, the least I can do is seal it up until I can get it fixed."

"Thanks, but I can manage." Disappointment made her tone sharp.

"Give me five minutes and I promise I won't bug you anymore. I need to explain some things."

Leigh hesitated. If he'd returned to worm himself back into her private life, she didn't want to hear it.

He pulled the flag back through the broken glass. "Just five minutes, Leigh."

She sighed and opened the door. "Come in." She picked up their mugs, and after emptying them, filled both with fresh coffee. When she turned around, she saw Nick standing on a chair, replacing the batteries in the smoke alert. She placed the cups on the table and closed the opened window.

Nick grinned at her. "I see what you mean about the kitchen gods."

She shrugged and sat down, motioning him to the other chair. He slipped off his jacket and draped it over the back of the chair before he seated himself.

Leigh took a bracing sip, then, cradling her mug in her hands, looked directly into his eyes. "You said you wanted to talk, so talk."

"First, as that famous character said, 'I don' know nothin' 'bout birthin' no babies'. Or, at least, I didn't until I read all those books before I brought them to you."

"But...but you said...what about your sisters? You said you—"

"I lied."

"What?"

"I was getting frustrated. I'd been trying for months to get you to go out with me. I couldn't seem to find the draw, the hook that would get you to say yes. Then you told me you were pregnant. I saw it as a chance to get close to you."

Leigh shook her head, wondering if it would help jostle her confused thoughts into order. "You mean pregnant women turn you on?"

"You turn me on, pregnant or not."

She gasped at his bluntness. "You're crazy!"

He grinned, his expression as wicked as the devil. "Probably. I can't explain it. There you sit, carrying someone else's baby, and all I can think of is how desirable you are. Of taking you to bed and loving you hot and sweet, long into the night."

Leigh felt her mouth drop open, and for a moment, for just an infinitesimal wild moment, longing swirled in her like a river released from winter ice. Then reality slammed into her. What he was talking about was an office affair. He wasn't talking about commitment or caring or even friends being lovers. He was talking straight old-fashioned lust.

Almost as if he could read her mind, he shook his head. "No, Leigh. I'm not trying to seduce you. I know you still have that other guy in your mind."

If he only knew, Leigh thought, her stomach clenching with anxiety. "I'm not looking for another lover, Nick."

"I know, but from now on, I'm going to be honest with you. I'm telling you up front you are the most attractive woman I've met in the past ten years."

Ten years? Then he wasn't talking about Darlene, his old high school sweetheart. It had to be the mysterious woman in his more recent past. Even so, she'd walked into one relationship based on hormones, and all the sweet talk in the world wasn't going to get her back into a no-win situation.

"I appreciate that, Nick, but—"

"I'm also asking you to let me be a friend. I want to help you, get to know you better." He flashed her a coaxing smile. "Besides, I never knew a woman who couldn't cook."

Leigh found herself wanting to believe him, wanting to believe they could have some kind of future together. And that wanting scared her to death.

"I don't know, Nick." She rose and walked out of the kitchen, aware he was following her. "I don't think it would work."

"What exactly do you imagine isn't going to work?"

She turned and faced him, her arms crossed protectively around her waist. "To start with, we don't have anything in common. You're lunch at the health store. I'm strictly Joe's Coney Island. You run five miles a day, and my idea of exercise is using the remote control. You're—"

"Hey, does the word *compromise* ring a bell?"

She tilted her head and quirked up the corner of her mouth. "What did you have in mind, that we jog around the corner to the local ice cream parlor?"

He shrugged. "Let's work it out, one step at a time. All I'm asking is that you give us the chance."

Leigh searched his face. He seemed sincere, she thought. Maybe he was, but she'd believed Brad was honest, too. *And maybe you'll never know unless you take this opportunity,* a tiny voice whispered in the back of her mind.

"Okay, Nick," she said with some reluctance. "But so help me, if you bring one more book into this house, I'll kick you out on your butt."

"Fair enough. Now I'm going to get the glass to fix the broken window."

He started toward the door, then paused, his eyes sparkling with humor. "How about a goodbye kiss?"

Laughter gurgled in her throat. "For a simple trip to the hardware store?"

"Why not? What can it hurt?"

In one step he was in front of her, the heat of his body warming her. Her gaze caught by his, she watched helplessly as he bent his head toward her. He slid his hands up her back, pulling her close against his hard frame. Her eyelids fluttered shut and she felt his touch, light as a butterfly's wings, against her mouth. The kiss was gentle, almost a query, and she instinctively slipped her arms around his neck.

Startled by her response, Nick felt pleasure slam through him. He lifted his head, gazing at the desire darkening her eyes. "That's enough to get me safely to my car," he whispered. "Now to ensure my safety on the roads..."

He bent his head, sealing his mouth against hers. Her taste was pure sweetness, and he eagerly sought more. Tilting her head to gain better access, he slipped the tip of his tongue along the edge of her lips, coaxing her into opening her mouth for his gentle invasion. He swept in, savoring the promise come true. She tasted like he'd always imagined, heady, intoxicating. He lost himself in the exploration of her mouth, delighted when her tongue fenced his in an everyone-wins duel.

Her memories hadn't been totally accurate, Leigh decided in a haze. She didn't remember him tasting this good, feeling this good. His rich male scent filled her head as his bold, searching tongue sent fiery waves down to the center of her body. Sharply aware of how their bodies molded together, her soft breasts crushed against his hard chest, she could only hold on to him as sensations swept over her. It was as if all her life had been directed toward this one moment.

When the kiss ended, she stared at him, unable to move and unwilling for it to end. He smiled and lightly brushed his lips over hers again in a movement that was curiously protective.

"That ought to keep me safe on my journey," he whispered.

His tone was husky and she thrilled at the thought that he might be as affected by the kiss as she had been. He pulled away from her with obvious reluctance and opened the front door.

"I'll be back in a few minutes." He stroked her cheek with the back of his fingers. "Meanwhile, you might start thinking about a hello kiss."

She watched him stride to his car, her heart pounding madly in her chest. *A hello kiss?* She was still trying to recover from the one they'd just shared. She closed the door and leaned against it. She had to be out of her mind to even consider setting herself up for a fall. On the other hand...

She felt a grin steal across her face. Another kiss from Nick *was* something to think about.

Five

The scene was perfect, one of Leigh's favorites. Soft balmy breezes, a golden tropical sun and a turquoise sea that gently curled along brilliant white sand. At the edge of the water she could see Nick, his muscular bronzed form gloriously nude. His searing gaze swept over her, and she felt a deep throb settle low in her belly. She knew she was running toward him, but she couldn't seem to get any closer. His wicked grin lured her. The tousled black curls on his forehead made her ache to bury her fingers deep in them, pulling his sensual mouth down on hers.

She watched as he lifted his lean, strong hand and waved at her before he sauntered into the foaming surf and disappeared beneath the waves.

"Nick!"

The sound of her cry awakened her and Leigh jerked upright. She glanced around her living room, disoriented for a moment, then realized she'd been napping. She flopped back against the throw pillow with a groan. Damn,

if she was going to have erotic dreams, why did they have
to end before she got to the good part?

Leigh shivered and nestled deeper under the afghan. She
glanced at the video recorder on top of the television and
saw the digital display was dark. Great. Still no electricity.
She stood and, keeping the knitted blanket tucked around
her, walked to the window.

The mid-afternoon sun sparkled on the layer of ice that
covered her lawn. The sleet storm Nick had warned her
about yesterday had come with a vengeance. She had to
admit the result was exquisite, each bush and tree sheathed
in a layer of crystal. But pretty as it was, she thought with
disgust, she was ready for the electricity to come back on.
She wasn't sure when she'd lost her power, but she'd
awakened to a cold house and would have traded her soul
for fifteen minutes of heat from her useless furnace.

She wandered into the kitchen and shook the teakettle.
With luck, she had enough water left for one cup. She cast
a disgusted look at the sink. She hoped her water pipes
hadn't burst. She chided herself for forgetting to leave water running when the forecast warned of freezing temperatures. Maybe she should consider spending the night in a
motel. She could always bunk down in the slightly warm
kitchen, but she'd be damned if she would go without water.

She turned on the flame. Thank God for gas, she
thought, as she spooned instant coffee into her mug. While
she waited for the water to boil, she mused about the previous day.

By the time Nick had returned from the hardware store,
she'd had second thoughts about their relationship. Somehow, it had seemed to be going too far, too fast. So when
he'd entered the house, bearing a potted yellow crocus he'd
bought from a sidewalk sale at the mall, she'd been careful
to be involved in a remodeling project.

Nick hadn't said anything about his promised hello kiss,
but Leigh remembered his knowing smile had sent a wave
of heat up her cheeks. Even worse, she'd spent the rest of
the day on tenterhooks waiting for him to kiss her again.

When he finally left, shortly after lunch, she'd been amazed at her disappointment as he went out of the door after merely brushing his mouth over her cheek. The empty loneliness of the long evening reminded her of the folly of building her expectations too high.

She was jarred back to the present by the whistling kettle just as the phone rang. Her heart skipped a beat, then Leigh felt herself grin. Nick just couldn't resist, she thought. Despite his assurances, he just had to call and check up on her.

Leigh grabbed the receiver as a thrill of mischief swirled through her.

"This had better be a pervert because if it's Nick Romano, you're doing it again."

"Uh . . . Leigh?"

"Oh, Maggie." Leigh could hear the bewilderment in her friend's voice and giggled. "I thought it was Nick monitoring me again."

"Again?"

"Yes, usually he's called me half a dozen times by now. Yesterday he and I had a big quarrel about it." Leigh cradled the phone against her shoulder as she poured hot water into her cup. "Honestly, you'd think pregnancy was a terminal illness from the way he keeps track of me."

"Ahh . . . that explains the weird call I just got from him."

"What weird call?"

Maggie laughed. "He wanted me to phone the staff and cancel work tomorrow. Then he asked if I'd offer to send Gene over with our four-wheel to bring you here for the night since you're without power."

"What?"

"Wait. It gets better. Then he suggested we set up some kind of schedule so all of us could take turns checking up on you."

Leigh clenched her teeth. "I hope you're kidding."

"Nope." Maggie said. "At least, I think that's what he had in mind. For a lawyer, he was remarkably vague."

Irritation jangled Leigh like ants crawling over her skin. "I'll kill him."

"Before you do, I'd like to know what is going on."

Leigh sighed and seated herself at the kitchen table. "Maggie, he's driving me crazy. He's always underfoot, and if he isn't here, he's calling at all hours to make sure I'm okay. He couldn't be worse if he..."

"If he knew the baby was his?"

Leigh bit her lower lip, unable to answer.

"I thought you promised to tell him about the baby," Maggie accused.

"Actually, I only promised to think about it."

"And...?"

"I'm still thinking."

Maggie gave an exasperated sigh. "What's to think about? You love him, don't you?"

"No...yes...oh, damn, I don't know, Maggie."

"Wait a minute. Let's take this a step at a time. What were you feeling about him at the Christmas party? I mean, you aren't the kind of woman to go to bed with a man simply because you're hot for him. Did you love him then?"

Leigh saw him in her memory's eye, funny, responsive, sexy. Had she loved him—or had she been lulled by the circumstances? No, she could honestly say, at the moment he had gently drawn her out of the crowded ballroom, she'd loved Nick.

"Yes," she whispered. She cleared her throat, then repeated more firmly. "At the time I was in love with him, but I'm not sure I loved him."

"Forgive me," Maggie drawled. "I'm from another generation. I never understood all this relevancy jazz. Exactly what is the difference between loving someone and being in love with him?"

"You saw him at the party, Maggie. When had you ever seen Nick like that? So relaxed and charming and...and..."

"Yes, I saw him. So you fell *in* love with Nick while he was half-lit and went to bed with him. What happened? Did you wake up and find him next to you, complete with three-piece suit, button-down collar and power tie?"

"Hardly," Leigh said with a chuckle. Then she sobered, rubbing her hand across her brow. "It was then I realized I didn't really know him and I had repeated the same mistake I'd made with Brad. The divorce made me wary about entering another relationship based strictly on physical attraction, but that's exactly what I did, isn't it? I just don't want to get in any deeper."

"So where does that leave you with Nick?"

Trust Maggie to ask tough questions, Leigh thought. "I don't know. So far, I don't see us having much in common."

"Well, for one thing, you share a baby," Maggie retorted. "Why not just level with him? Tell him everything in a calm, collected manner. You might be surprised. Maybe he loves you."

Leigh wanted to believe her. She wanted to believe that the minute she told Nick the truth, love would blossom between them like a full-blown rose. But she'd gone far beyond being calm and collected about Nick. And she'd stopped believing in fairy tales during her marriage.

And what about him? He made it obvious he cared about her, but in what way? As a co-worker who was in trouble? As a friend? A potential lover? After all, he hadn't even asked her out for an honest-to-God date since he found out she was pregnant.

"Leigh? Yo, Leigh. Are you there?"

Maggie's tone told Leigh she had missed whatever Maggie had been saying to her.

"Sorry, I was thinking."

"Look, I'm sorry I poked my nose into your business. I know you'll do whatever you think is best for you."

"It's okay, Maggie. It helps me to know I can bounce ideas off you if I need to."

"Yes, well . . . before we get all mushy, would you like to stay here until you get your power back?"

Leigh shook her head, driving all thoughts of Nick from her mind. "No, thanks. It's stupid to have Gene on these roads when there's a bunch of motels near here. I'll call around until I find a room and stay the night. I'm sure I'll have my electricity back on by tomorrow."

"Okay, but feel free to call if you can't find a room."

"I'll be fine, Maggie. Enjoy your extra day off. See you Tuesday."

Leigh hung up the receiver and drained the last of her coffee. She darted a glance at her battery-operated kitchen clock. Three-thirty. If she was going to find a motel room for the night, she'd better get moving. For an instant she was strongly tempted to call Nick—take him up on his of-fer to help. But hadn't she promised herself last night she wouldn't have expectations about Nick? No, she was able to make arrangements for herself without Nick.

She nodded approval at winning the silent argument and went looking for her telephone book.

"Listen, car, if you'll only start, I promise I'll get you a nice tune-up next weekend."

Leigh felt like a fool trying to sweet talk her fifteen-year-old Chevy into starting, but she was running out of time. She'd been able to find an available motel room in the area, and the bored voice on the other end of the phone had said that with the emergency, it was strictly first come, first serve. Although it had taken her only a few minutes to throw some essentials into a bag, she had spent almost an hour chipping the ice off her door enough to get it open. Every time she'd breathed on her chilled fingers to warm them, she'd cursed the lack of hot water that would have sped up the job. With the chemical defroster, she'd been able to clear her windows in minutes, but it looked as if no power or promise on earth was going to get her frozen engine to turn over.

She twisted the key once more and winced at the slow, grinding sound. Great. Now her battery was weakening. Exasperated, she yanked the key from the ignition and shoved open the door. She stepped out of the seat in time to see a dark green Jeep Cherokee pull into her drive. Nick exited the Jeep and walked toward her, carrying a silver Thermos flask.

"Hi," he said as he paced carefully on the slick con-crete. "Any chance I can bum some coffee from you?"

She laughed. "You came all this way to borrow coffee?"

"Actually, I've been out all day helping drivers. It's something I learned to do up north on bad snow days, when I was in college. I've been out of coffee for an hour, and when I saw I was in your neighborhood, I thought you might be good for a fill-up."

"Uh-huh. And what about your call to Maggie? Didn't we agree that I would let you know if I needed help?"

"And I didn't phone you," he said with a self-satisfied smile. "I called Maggie. *She* called you, so you can't say I broke my word. Now, about that coffee?"

"Uh...sure." Leigh had to hand it to Nick. Trust a lawyer to find a loophole.

"In fact," she said, unwilling to get into a semantics argument with him. "How about a trade? I can't give you coffee, but I'll put some soup in the thermos for you."

He arched an eyebrow. "What do I have to do?"

"Get my car going so I can get to a motel."

"A motel? You don't intend to drive on this stuff, do you? Why don't you—" He threw up his hands as she opened her mouth. "I know, I know," he said with a trace of wry humor. "I'm doing it again. Butting in where I haven't been asked." He handed her the flask. "The correct answer is, you've got yourself a deal."

She laughed and walked into the house. By the time she had filled his jug and gone back outside, she saw Nick had maneuvered his car so it was nose-to-nose with hers and connected by jumper cables. He looked up at her approach.

"Good, you're back. Hop in the Cherokee and rev it up. I need a little more power."

She slid behind the steering wheel, placed the two thermoses behind the driver's seat and eased down on the accelerator until Nick signaled. She took a moment to look around the roomy compartment as he worked under her car's hood. She hadn't known he owned anything except his sedan and the thought of a conservative Nick with something like a Jeep intrigued her.

She smelled perfume, a faint floral scent that tantalized her nostrils and she saw a tube of lipstick on the dashboard. Startled, she flashed a glance at Nick. Was that why he had left yesterday after lunch? Had he had a date last night?

She told herself it didn't matter, but she knew she lied. It mattered...a lot. She caught a glimpse of Nick through the windshield, both thumbs raised in victory. She gave him a wavering smile and tried to push down a sense of betrayal as she joined him beside her roughly running car.

Nick threw his arm around her shoulders and gave her a hug. "Once again, medical science triumphs," he said with a chuckle as he waved a metal can in front of her. "Ether. A few drops in your carburetor and it'll start, no matter how cold the weather. Your engine needs about five minutes to warm up, so get in and keep her going."

"I can't believe a naturalist like you would use something like ether," she said after she'd slid into the seat and cranked down the window. "What about the environment?"

"Hey, I didn't use an aerosol, did I? When you're ready, take off and I'll follow you to make sure you get there safely."

He coiled up the cables and stored them in the back of the Jeep. Despite the slippery conditions, his movements were a symphony of motion. Her palms itched to cup his hips just as she had the night they'd made love. She remembered how he'd gazed down on her, his eyes slumberous and smoky with passion as he loomed over her in the bed. His touch, so magical, had teased her into a frenzy and each movement of his body had—

The sound of a car horn jarred her out of her daydream and she saw two vehicles slide into each other. She watched, appalled, as both drivers attempted to drive on, their rear tires spinning madly. She stepped out of her car and ignored the biting wind as she observed Nick help the drivers disengage their vehicles. Even as they drove down the street, Leigh saw them sliding on the slick surface.

For the first time she doubted the wisdom of driving to the motel. If she had an accident, she could hurt the baby. She chewed on the corner of her mouth, torn between staying in a house with no heat or water and risking the roads. Troubled, she looked at Nick as he returned to her side, his expression grim.

"It's like that all over the city," he said. "Too many people in this town have no idea how to drive on ice." He tucked her muffler more securely around her throat. "Let's go. I don't want you to drive after dark. It will be even worse then."

She resisted cuddling her face into the warmth of his hands. "I've changed my mind. Will you drive me to the motel in your car?"

She didn't want him to think she was unable to take care of herself, but still . . . Well, if he wanted to say "I told you so," she'd have to take it. She had to think about her baby's safety.

Nick gave her a casual smile. "Sure. No sense in you driving when the four-wheel is available."

Leigh felt a sense of relief. At least Nick wasn't going to gloat. By the time he had her and her bag tucked away in the Cherokee, she was relaxed, confident that Nick was going to keep within his boundaries. A glimpse of the smug smile on Nick's face gave her a twinge of worry. Just what was on his mind?

Nick flung open the door of his apartment, tossed his jacket over the back of the couch and placed Leigh's small overnight case on the floor.

"I, for one, am glad the room had already been taken. That place looked too seedy for even cockroaches to be willing to stay," he said. "Here we are—home, sweet home." He turned to welcome Leigh, but the doorway was empty.

"Leigh?"

She peered around the jamb, her expression wary. "I've got a bad feeling about this. It smells like leather and . . . and . . ."

Nick looked around his living room, trying to see it as she did. It looked like a standard room to him. Comfortable furniture, easy-care carpet and drapes, and a couple of paintings that were expensive but tasteful. "That's just the furniture. There aren't any whips or chains, so what do you find so threatening, Leigh?" He walked back to the door, gently pulled her in and closed it, snapping the lock. She visibly jumped at the sound. "Don't you like my color scheme?"

Leigh gave him a baleful glare. "You know damn well it isn't your apartment. I'm just not sure it's a good idea that I spend the night here."

"Was it my fault the motel room was rented out? What were your options? You couldn't go home, and unless you wanted to spend the rest of the night phoning around town for a room, the most logical thing to do was stay in my guest room." The clean, womanly scent on her hair tickled his nose as he eased her coat from her shoulders and laid her jacket next to his.

"Hmm."

Nick ignored her distrustful expression as he walked into the kitchen separated from the main area by a counter, flipped on the light and opened his freezer. "Make yourself at home. You like lasagna, don't you? I know you and Maggie usually eat lunch at that little Italian place in the Main Street Mall."

From the corner of his eye, he could see her standing, hesitant, in the center of the room as he placed a frozen, precooked lasagna in the microwave. He hummed as he chopped vegetables for a salad, aware of Leigh when she finally moved. Without being obvious, he watched as she removed her boots and began wandering through the room. He figured her curious nature would have her poking around.

Leigh couldn't help it. She was impressed by his apartment. Of course she'd known Nick liked good living, but she had never expected anything like this. The quiet elegance of his decor struck an unexpected chord in her. The rich smell of the leather furniture added a masculine aura she appreciated. She explored the spacious room, noting that all the paintings on the wall were by Native American artists.

"You put your money where your mouth is, don't you?" she said.

"What do you mean?"

She nodded at the artwork. "I knew you contributed money to the fine arts, but I guess I figured it was just a tax write-off."

He laughed as he tossed a salad. "No, my folks took me to powwows when I was a kid, and Indian art always fascinated me."

"It shows."

She continued ambling as he involved himself in his cooking. His decorating style was definitely different from hers, but she didn't feel out of place. In fact, she suspected she would enjoy spending a lot of time in his apartment, and she hurriedly avoided the thought.

"What do you think?"

She looked at him, startled by his sudden question. "About what?"

He nodded at the area. "Do you like it?"

"Oh...yes. It's a lot like you...solid, dependable." She examined the photographs on the mantelpiece. "Your family?"

"Yes, and a few friends."

She picked up a photograph of an extremely attractive woman. Leigh resented that she felt ordinary when confronted with the woman's sultry expression and pouty mouth. She wondered if this was the woman from his past and fought to keep her envy from showing. "Is this one of your sisters?" she asked, unable to resist.

"No, that's Linda. She and I were study partners in law school together. She dropped out to become a model. She and her husband are in Europe for the winter."

He wondered at the peculiar expression, almost one of relief, that crossed her face. What was she thinking? Was it possible she might be jealous? He suppressed a smile at the thought. The very idea of Leigh being jealous delighted him, but common sense told him he was indulging in wishful thinking.

He took two glasses off the rack and removed a bottle of Riesling from the refrigerator. "How about something to drink?"

"Sure," she said and seated herself on a stool across from him. "Riesling is my favorite."

He smiled, then reached for a bottle that had been hidden behind the wine. "Then we'll have it after your baby's born. For right now, how about some sparkling grape juice."

She gave him a mock grimace. "Okay, you tyrant." She sipped on her juice and wished her kitchen had the working space his did. She especially liked how well lighted the area was and marveled at his state-of-the-art appliances. She could tell he was a man who took his cooking seriously. Fascinated, she watched him skillfully slice through some tomatoes. "God, you're fast with that knife."

He brandished the cutlery. "Just a little something I learned from a Japanese chef. It's all in the wrists."

She laughed and an inner tension Nick hadn't realized he had relaxed. That's what he'd wanted, Leigh comfortable in his home. All he had to do was keep things friendly, and Leigh might come closer to recognizing they belonged together. Of course, the trick was staying casual.

The sight of her brown hair, tousled in soft curls around her shoulders, and her long, slender legs, emphasized by her soft, worn jeans, made that difficult; but nothing fortitude, endurance and a cold shower couldn't handle.

"Can I help?"

For a moment he thought she was making an offer he couldn't refuse, but as she nodded toward the food he had ready to serve, he understood she wanted to assist with dinner.

"You can set out the dishes. You don't mind eating at the counter, do you?"

Her laughter enchanted him. "It'll be like eating at a diner. All we need is a jukebox."

He went to the stereo and turned it on. The mellow sounds of a popular Italian tenor filled the room.

"Of course, it's not Conway Twitty," he teased.

"That's okay. It fits the mood."

Nick wanted to ask what mood she was feeling, but was afraid to push. The few minutes needed to get dinner finished passed in a companionable silence. He watched as she took her first bite. Her eyes widened in surprise, and she stared at her plate.

"This is great. Is it all vegetable?"

He grinned and picked up his own fork. "Yes, the secret is I use my own canned tomatoes. Even my mother, who is pure Italian, says it isn't too bad...for vegetarian lasagna. So you really like it?"

"Ambrosia. Where did you learn to cook like this?"

"Are you kidding? With four sisters, you'd think I wouldn't have to cook. But my mother is a big believer in men doing their share of housekeeping chores. Once I started cooking, I found I really loved doing it. Pretty soon my sisters were bribing me to take their turn at the stove."

"I can understand their reasoning. Any chance I could bribe you to cook for me?"

"Sweetheart, I'm already cooking for you." Her eyes widened and he forced himself not to smile. "Bread?" he said, handing her the plate.

She chose a piece, relief obvious on her face. "And you did a wonderful job. This is delicious."

Lord, he thought, he was making her every statement, no matter how innocent, sound so provocative. If he didn't stop, he would spook her permanently. Nick slammed a lid hard on that thought. Time to get the conversation in a normal channel. "Tell me about growing up on a dairy farm," he said, desperately.

He tried to focus on her words, but all he could really hear was the musical sound of her voice. He loved watching her expressive face, emotions passing over it like sunlight chasing shadows across the land. Every time she moved, her knees nudged his, sending streaks of fire to his groin.

Inwardly he groaned. Maybe she was right. Maybe it wasn't such a good idea to have her stay the night. He realized he hadn't been listening to her and tuned her in with effort.

"...at least Dad was a good sport about having all his cows named after the Nashville Hall of Fame."

"Sounds like you grew up in a loving home."

Her eyes turned misty. "Yes, I really miss them."

He hated the sadness in her expression and searched for a way to banish it. "Want some more?" he said as he gestured at the lasagna.

She looked at the casserole with confusion, then shook her head.

"Okay, you wash, I'll dry." He rose and started collecting the dirty dishes.

She stared at him a moment, then giggled. "Don't you have a dishwasher?"

"Yes, that's why I'm drying. You'll have to do all the work loading the dishwasher."

"But I'm a guest," she said teasingly, as she stacked the dishes on the rack while he started the coffeemaker.

"Hey, I'm an equal-opportunity employer. I cooked, you clean. But to show you what a nice guy I am, I'll start a fire and we can have coffee in front of it."

As he lighted the wood in the hearth, he was conscious of her movement in the kitchen. He crouched in front of the fire and watched as the fragrant apple wood smoldered, then burst into flames. It felt right—the crackling fire, the smell of brewing coffee, the sense of a snug house barricaded against the winter's cold. Just the two of them sharing a quiet evening at home. Nick felt a tightness in his throat. Never had he wanted such a oneness, a completeness with any woman as he did right now with Leigh.

"Nick?"

He tore his gaze from the spell of the flames and saw her standing in front of him, coffee mugs in her hands. The light from the fire touched her hair with gold and softened the curves of her figure. She gave him a quizzical smile and he smiled back. He rose from the floor and took one of the mugs from her.

He stood facing her, watching her over the rim of his cup as he sipped the hot liquid. He explored her face with hunger. In the background, the singer crooned a slow, sensuous ballad, and the invitation in Leigh's eyes drew Nick like a Siren's call. He took the cup from her unresisting fingers and placed it with his on the mantel.

"May I have this dance?" To his own ears, his voice was husky, filled with the dark sorcery she wove around him.

He slowly pulled her into his arms and, cuddling her soft body against him, guided her around the space between the fireplace and the sofa. After a moment's hesitation, she seemed to melt into him. He spanned her waist with his hands, resisting the urge to press her pliant body against his rigid ache. Then he felt her arms slip around his neck, the heat of her breasts on his chest, and he was lost. He groaned and buried his lips in the fragrant silk of her neck. Her taste was all woman, intoxicating and sensuous. He nibbled his way along her jaw until he could reach his final goal, the sweet mystery of her mouth.

She moaned, and the sound of it filled him with exultation. She wanted him—wanted him as much as he wanted her. With that knowledge, he demanded entry into her mouth, and when she opened her lips to him, he swept in like a conqueror. Her tongue dared his for dominance, and he savored the spicy taste of her challenge.

Slowly he eased her onto the sofa. As he feverishly pulled her sweatshirt over her head, she opened the buttons on his shirt and tangled her fingers in his hair. Her moist, hot mouth on his chest sent urgent messages to his hardening body.

"How did you get this mark?" she asked, running the tip of her finger down the long, thin scar on his chest.

"It's an old war injury." He gasped as her tongue tasted him.

"What war?"

"The war of the sexes," he muttered, distracted as he flicked open the front fastener of her bra. He held his breath when he cupped her lush, firm breasts and saw their perfection, all rose and ivory.

"Did you win?" Her voice was husky, sultry and her eyes cloudy with desire.

He brushed his thumbs over the peaks, his body tightening as he watched her nipples draw up into stiff, hard buds. A shaft of pure male satisfaction surged through him when she closed her eyes with a soft moan.

"Not until today." He caressed her again, reveling in her response. "Oh, God, Leigh. You are so beautiful," he whispered. "Not in all my dreams did I ever imagine such beauty."

He bent his head and kissed the smooth pale flesh. Her taste burst on his tongue, and he caressed the satin skin around the crests, deliberately delaying what he knew they both wanted. She threw back her head, her breathing fast and shallow.

"Nick," she moaned and her plea drove him on.

He drew the taut nipple into his mouth and suckled her gently. She clutched him tightly to her and reality blurred. There was only the scent of her, the taste of her . . . the feel of her. He couldn't get enough. Her fingers, buried deep in his hair, tugged at him and he complied with her unspoken demand. He kissed his way back to her hot, wet mouth.

"So sweet . . . you feel so good," he muttered against her lips. "All fire and . . . satin and . . . Oh, God, Leigh. Sweetheart . . ." He groaned as she arched her hips against him.

She tugged at his shirt and he helped her, desperate for the feel of her breasts against his naked skin. Her light, flowery scent was driving him wild.

"Oh, angel. If only you . . ."

Vaguely, he became aware something had changed. He searched for her lips again, but she turned her head away from him, her body stiff beneath him. He looked up and saw a stricken expression in her eyes.

"Leigh?"

She averted her gaze. "Please stop, Nick."

He couldn't believe it. How could she deny what was happening between them? Frustration and anger poured through him, and he jerked to a sitting position, fighting the urge to shake her. She sat up, crossing her arms over her breasts, her face hidden by her tumbled hair.

He saw the vulnerability, the pain in the way she huddled on the sofa and realized something more basic than denying their mutual passion was hurting her. He closed his eyes and took a deep breath. He fought down his desire and moved back from her, instinctively recognizing her need for space.

"Leigh, what happened?" he said softly. "Was I wrong? Didn't you want me as much as I wanted you?"

She brought her knees up to her chest and curled into what was clearly a defensive posture in a corner of the sofa. She swept her hair back from her face and took a shuddering breath. "No, you weren't wrong," she whispered. "I did want you."

"Then what happened? Why did you suddenly pull away from me?" For a moment he thought she wasn't going to answer.

"I've been through this before," she said, her gaze focused on the fire. "The wanting . . . the needing."

He remained silent, sensing there was more.

"It burns through you like a flash fire," she continued. "But when the flame dies, all that's left is ashes."

"You mean the baby's father."

She shrugged. "Not him. My ex-husband." She looked at him, her expression shuttered. "Look, I married Brad because he was exciting and challenging. Every girl on campus wanted him, and I was crazy in love with him."

Nick inwardly flinched. He didn't want to hear this, but knew it was somehow the key to Leigh. "Then you married him."

She relaxed slightly against the back of the sofa, her solemn gaze on him.

"Oh, he tried to talk me into going to bed with him, but the way I was raised, premarital sex was out. So we got married."

"What went wrong?"

"For a while, nothing. The biggest problem we had was money. He didn't have any, and all I had was a small trust fund from my grandparents. Soon, it seemed to make sense to use the money for his degree while I worked to support us. I mean, after all, we were working for the same future, weren't we?"

"And you bought that?"

She shrugged, flashing him a wry grin. "I did protest some, but he only had to lure me to bed, and all our arguments seemed to be petty." She paused and Nick remained quiet, willing to give her time to search out her memories. "Then one afternoon, shortly after his graduation, I got sent home from work early due to a kitchen fire at the café. He was home, in bed . . . with . . ."

"The bastard!" Nick muttered, reaching for her.

She flinched back and shook her head. "No, don't touch me. I need to finish this. Then maybe you'll understand why . . ." She took a deep shuddering breath. "After the divorce, I realized I'd spent two and a half years of my life serving a selfish man as his financial support and housekeeper with sexual favors, favors I'd been sharing with other women. My marriage, my money, my chance at my future were gone because I let my desire overcome my good sense. I took secretarial training so I could work and put myself through college. I'd always wanted to be a lawyer and I planned that nothing, no one would stop me from reaching my goal. I promised myself I would never enter another relationship based on physical attraction again, but . . ."

She stroked her hand over her still flat abdomen, her gaze centered on the fire again, and Nick felt a sharp stab of jealousy rage through him.

"And because of the baby's father, you don't trust yourself. You think all you and I have together is a sexual attraction and that scares you." A guilty expression crossed her face, and he forced himself not to reach for her, to hold her close in comfort as he wanted to hold her.

"No," she whispered, so low he had to lean forward to hear her. "What I feel for you is so much stronger than I felt for Brad. So much . . .'' She closed her eyes and shuddered. ''And that frightens me.''

He took her chin firmly in her hand, forcing her to look at him. ''Leigh, I care about you and I can understand your wariness. I won't rush you. I'll give you the time you need to work this out. Just know, I don't intend to step away from what's happening between us.''

She searched his face, and he sensed she wanted to tell him something important, but didn't know if she could trust him. Or maybe, he thought, she doubted herself.

He ran his thumb along her lips, still swollen from his kisses, and sighed. ''I think we'd better call it a night. It might be safer.''

She gave him a tremulous smile and he rose from the couch. He heard the rustle of her clothing as he picked up her suitcase. When he turned back to her, her sweatshirt was back on and she was standing, watchful of his next move. He walked to the guest room with her and placed her suitcase on the bed before he returned to the open doorway.

''Sleep well. And don't worry. I only allow myself one seduction attempt a night.''

She smiled wanly at his feeble joke. ''Thanks, Nick...for everything.''

He knew she wasn't talking about just a place for the night. He smiled, wishing he dared taste her one more time, then shut the door behind him. He walked into the kitchen and poured himself a well-deserved brandy. The smooth, acrid tang of the cordial couldn't erase the memory of her, but helped sooth his jagged nerves. Somehow, he'd gained a little tonight, he thought. Not only did Leigh want him, she trusted him. Otherwise she wouldn't have opened up to him as she had. And she definitely wouldn't be staying the night, even in separate beds. He gently swirled the liquid in the glass. Yes, things seemed to be moving right along. And he laughed to himself with sheer joy as he downed the last of the brandy.

Six

___

Nick tapped lightly on the closed door and eased it open after getting no response. He placed the small tray he carried on the dresser and sat on the edge of the bed.

Leigh lay under the covers, curled in a ball. The early-morning light warmed the rich sable color of her hair and gave it golden highlights. Nick felt his insides twist at the sight of her face, softened by sleep. Her skin glowed in the dim sunlight like a rare pink pearl, her long dark lashes contrasting with the wild rose blush in her cheeks.

Nick brushed an errant curl off her forehead. Curious how different she looked asleep, he thought. She looked less guarded, more approachable. And so beautiful.

Unable to resist, he bent and brushed his mouth across her soft shoulder. A tiny smile tugged at her lips as she wiggled onto her back. Encouraged by her smile, Nick took advantage of her new position and kissed her tempting mouth. Her sweet taste burst on his tongue as her eyelids fluttered.

"Wake up, Sleeping Beauty. You're missing the best part of the day." He sat back as she looked around the room.

"Good morning," she said with a sleepy-eyed smile.

She stretched her arms above her head and the sheet slipped, exposing the tops of her rounded breasts. Nick gasped. *Oh, Lord. She's naked!* The blanket, trapped under his hip, pulled taut around her body and outlined every delicious curve. He groaned, gripped her shoulders, and sealed his mouth over hers. He meant for the kiss to be tender, a simple good-morning kiss, but the feel of her satin skin under his fingers, the excitement of her mouth opening to his lips and tongue overcame his intentions. And when she returned his flame with her own fire, there was no way he could stop. Her fingers at the nape of his neck sent primitive shivers down his spine and he had to have more.

"Oh, God, Leigh...sweetheart—" he muttered. With his mouth, he traced a path along her cheek and down her jaw where he could spend a lifetime nibbling on the delicate lobe. Her trembling response and her excited little cries drove him on. He licked the tight cord in her throat and teased the soft upper curves of her breasts. "I could make a feast of you."

He lifted his gaze and stared at her face, her mouth swollen with his kisses, her hair tousled and wanton. He captured her gaze with his as he eased the blanket to her waist and cupped her breasts with a gentle touch. He felt her nipples bead under his stroking thumb. Elation swept through him as she closed her eyes and moaned. No matter how she might deny it, she belonged to him. Her reaction proved it.

He bent and took one of the hard nipples in his mouth, curling his tongue around it. He gently raked his teeth over the peak as he drew it deeper. Her hands clutched his head and pressed him closer to her breast.

"Nick...oh, Nick...please..."

He lifted his head, pleased at the look of craving he'd put on her face.

"Please what, Leigh?" He watched as his breath across her wet skin caused the nipple to draw up even tighter. "Do you want me, Leigh? Say it. I want to hear you say you want me, Leigh.''

He stretched out on top of her, cradling his hardness between her thighs. Even through the bed linens, he could feel the heart of her and he rotated his hips slowly. ''Is this what you want, sweetheart? A slow, lazy morning loving? We have all the time in the world to make it leisurely and caring or hot and greedy. I want to be deep inside you, burning us both up.''

His words twined through her half-conscious mind like smoke. Her body felt languorous, throbbing with a sweet ache everywhere his hands touched her. Her consciousness whispered a warning, but she didn't want to hear. Instead, she listened to the sensual message of her senses. She shivered as she felt his mouth, hot and wet, on her breast. His gentle suckling drew a thread of tension between her nipple and womb and she moaned, almost unable to stand the pleasure. As his long, warm fingers moved toward the aching center of her femininity, reality slammed through her. The whispered warning became a full-blown alert and chased away the last wisps of her sensual fog. Suddenly, her failure to tell him the truth about the baby became a betrayal, and she flinched from the knowledge. No, she couldn't think of Nick as the father. She forced away the erotic demands of her body. Nor could she afford to think of him as a lover. Then what was she doing, allowing herself to encourage him in his seduction?

A rosy color crept up her face, and Nick realized she'd become fully awake, fully aware of her vulnerability. She pushed weakly against his shoulders. ''Nick, please stop. We can't do this.''

Her hesitant voice told him she wanted him as much as he wanted her, but that something stopped her. He stroked his hand down to the nest of curls between her legs. ''Yes, we can, sweetheart. There's only you and me and this bed. Don't fight it, Leigh. Don't fight yourself.''

''I thought you promised you weren't going to seduce me,'' she said with a nervous laugh.

His painful hardness demanded fulfillment, but panic lurked in the back of her eyes, and Nick knew she was trying to defuse the passion between them with humor. He rested his forehead against her shoulder, his hands gripping her waist tightly as he fought to subdue the raging need in him. Torn between his aching body and a new sense of protectiveness, Nick resigned himself to backing off. If she needed more time, he'd give it to her.

"That was last night's seduction attempt. Now is this morning's. And if you play your cards right, maybe I'll do another one for lunch." He gave her a quick peck on the cheek and rolled over to sit on the edge of the bed. He cupped her face in his hand, forcing her gaze to meet his. "But there will come a time, Leigh, when neither of us will be able to stop."

She watched him with solemn eyes and he smiled. He pulled the sheet up and tucked it under her arms, covering her tempting breasts. "Now, since I don't have any crackers, I brought you some toast and tea. My sisters swear by it for morning sickness."

He forced himself to keep his voice casual while he handed her her robe and retrieved the tray. He kept his gaze carefully averted, giving her time to get covered and into a sitting position before he laid the tray across her lap. He resumed his seat and watched as she fingered the stalk of celery in the bud vase, a smile tugging at the corners of her mouth.

"I know it should be a flower," he said, winking at her. "But I seem to have run out of roses."

She laughed. "At least it's not broccoli. I hate broccoli." She picked up a slice of toast and examined it, frowning. "I've never seen melba toast look like this."

"I made it myself. And before you ask, the tea is chamomile—good for calming the stomach."

Leigh shook her head. "Don't you trust anything from the grocery store? I know for a fact commercial melba is low fat, low sodium and low taste. Why do you have to make your own?"

"Because the commercial stuff has preservatives to prolong its shelf life. And never mind distracting me with another argument on our different life-styles."

She looked sheepish and he grinned. "I'm getting used to your tactics, Leigh. For some reason, you want to keep barriers between us, but I'm not going to let you. However long it takes, I'll wait for you to admit you want me as much as I want you."

He watched her shuttered expression as she crumbled the toast with restless fingers. He slipped a piece of toast between her lips. "Now, eat up. I've got plans for today."

"What plans? What's the weather like?" she mumbled around the bite.

He leaned back and clasped his hands around one bent knee. "The sleet stopped around midnight and the prediction is for warming temperatures. With luck, the roads will clear by noon. I can't get through to the power company, but the radio says there is still a lot of power outages."

She grimaced. "I hope I get my electricity back soon. And I better find out about my water."

"I'm baby-sitting a couple of horses for a friend of mine and I need to go feed them. I thought you might like to go with me. We could check out your house on the way."

"Horses?" Her expression brightened and he laughed.

"I guess that means you're interested in going." He patted her hip, and his hand lingered on the firm curve. Her scent, heady, delicate, all woman, drifted around his head in a sensual cloud. He felt himself drowning in the golden flecks of her irises and fought against the surge of desire that flowed through him. He had to get out of there or he would do something he regretted—no matter how much he would enjoy it. He rose in a sudden move, jostling the liquid in her cup. "Uh, I'll have breakfast ready when you're dressed."

She grabbed the teetering cup and watched in amazement as he hurried out of the room. *What the devil?* She closed her eyes and groaned. Where was her mind? When she'd first opened her eyes, the sight of him had been a continuation of her dream-filled night. He'd been there, male, sexy, that tiny scar in the corner of his mouth beguiling her. And when he kissed her, it hadn't been any hardship to join in. After all, wasn't this what she'd done all night—dreamt of being held tight in his arms, his mouth hot and hungry against hers? And she had to admit, despite all her promises to herself, she got a jolt of satisfaction that she could affect him.

So? You've always known you could turn him on, she told herself crossly. Isn't that what had gotten her into this mess in the first place? One prod from her hormones, and she'd gone to bed with a man who mourned another woman.

She set the tray on the end of the bed and swung her feet off the mattress. *Thank God, no nausea.* She went to the dresser and, stripping off her robe, peered at her reflection in the mirror. So far, there hadn't been too many changes from her pregnancy. Her breasts were fuller, more tender, but her waist was still slim, even if there was that slight bulge. She tightened her stomach muscles, but couldn't suck in the slight roundness. She shrugged and relaxed, once again examining herself. Yes, she supposed Nick *could* be interested in her, but she found it suspicious that she had worked with him for two years without one pass from him. Yet the minute he finds out she's pregnant, he is overcome with desire. *Right,* she thought derisively. What kind of normal male claims to be interested in a woman he thinks is pregnant with another man's baby? She observed her cynical expression. So what was his motive?

She wandered into the bathroom and started her morning routine. Okay, so where did she stand? She knew Nick had a woman in his past, someone who haunted him. *Haunted! That's it.* Maybe the mysterious Cara was dead, and Nick was only using Leigh as a substitute. Leigh stared at her stunned reflection in the bathroom mirror, vaguely aware of her toothbrush dangling from her mouth. Could that be it?

She rinsed away the toothpaste, then stepped into the shower and let the warm water caress her as she sorted through her thoughts. She could see it from Nick's point of

view. He couldn't have the woman he wanted, but Leigh
was available. There was plenty of sexual attraction between them, so there wouldn't be any problem there. And,
since she was pregnant, without any hope of marriage with
the father, no doubt he thought she would be glad to marry
anyone who would accept her child. A bitter laugh forced
itself out of her. He'd probably even figured he would be
able to keep his top-notch secretary.

Leigh turned the water off and jerked a towel from the
rack. Well, she'd be damned if she'd hand him a ready-
made family just because she was pregnant. Maybe he was
willing to settle for second choice, but she wasn't. She'd be
primo or nothing. And that wouldn't be until she was admitted to the bar. So, the first thing she needed to do was
get the hell out of this apartment. It would be all too easy
to nourish his fantasy if they spent much time here, playing house.

Of course, Nick wasn't the only one who had been living with illusion, was he? Hadn't she been putting off the
decision she needed to make about the baby? Desolation
swept through her, and Leigh leaned against the vanity, her
eyes closed against the pain. How could she ever give up her
baby? Nick's baby? But what was the alternative? Raising
a child would make demands on her she wasn't sure she
could meet. What if she began to resent the baby? What if
she— *No!* She drew in a deep breath and, straightening,
stared at her determined image in the mirror. Adoption was
the best thing for the baby and for her. Ruthlessly she
pushed away her doubts. She would ask her obstetrician
how to start proceedings, when she saw him this week.
Nodding in determination, Leigh headed back into the
bedroom.

I must be some kind of wimp, Leigh thought, looking
around her bedroom. No, Nick's guest room, she reminded herself. Just because her things were scattered all
over the place was no reason to think of it as her room. And
what happened to her determination not to play house with

Nick? She frowned at her reflection in the mirror. Here it was Friday and she was still staying at Nick's apartment.

Oh, everyone thought it great she had someplace to live while she waited for power to be restored to her house. Maggie even pointed out she could hardly afford to stay at a motel, not with the expense of replacing her burst water pipes and repairing her water-damaged kitchen. But she knew the real reason why she hadn't moved out.

The past week had been a voyage of exploration. Nick had been quite open in the fact he was wooing her. Leigh smiled. What a wonderfully old-fashioned word—and she was very much in favor of the practice. It had meant candlelight dinners and dancing. There had been roses on her desk and a night at the theater. Nick had even gone to a square dance with her. His enthusiasm for learning the intricate movements had left her weak with laughter. So each day she had stayed and fallen more under his spell.

Leigh sighed and unwound the towel wrapped around her damp hair, running her fingers through it. She heard the doorbell chime, but ignored it as she turned on her blow-dryer. She *had* to get out of here. Not because of Nick, but because she was getting too used to having him around, and she didn't trust that feeling. She'd reached the point where she didn't want to leave...ever. And that was dangerous for her mind, for her heart.

Leigh set aside the dryer, and the sound of chimes interrupted her thoughts. Nick was probably in the shower, so she'd better answer the door. She shrugged into her scarlet satin robe and went to open it. A slender woman with a colorful sombrero perched on her head, rakishly tilted over her face, stood with a hand poised to knock on the door.

"Buenos dias, Senor Nick," the woman crooned in sultry tones. "Buy a margarita for a thirsty woman?"

Her voice caught in her throat, Leigh could only gape. She recognized the subtle scent of the woman's perfume. She'd been smelling it in the Cherokee for a week. This had to be one of Nick's... friends. Maybe even— Leigh silently groaned. God, she was obsessed with the unknown Cara. Even worse than Nick.

The stranger lifted her gaze, and her laughter choked off when she saw Leigh. "Oops. I thought you were Nick." Her face flushed a bright pink. "Is he here?"

Leigh found herself vaguely glad she'd embarrassed the unknown woman. She examined the classic features. It wasn't fair that she had to compete with Julia Roberts's twin—especially when she stood there without a speck of makeup, Leigh thought crossly. Well, no woman with a knock-'em-dead figure was going to make her feel unfeminine.

"I'm sorry, he's in the...bedroom right now." She saw the woman's gaze take note of her appearance, and Leigh purposely leaned against the door, trying to look like a woman who had spent all afternoon in bed with the world's most exciting man. Let the bimbo wonder about that for a while. "May I tell him who's calling?" she drawled.

The other woman's face flushed a deeper red, and she started backing away. "Uh...uh, no. I seem to have stopped at a bad time. I'll just—"

"Kelsey, dear! When did you get back? Where's Dave?" Nick walked across the living room, his wildly disordered hair still damp from his shower. His open shirt hung over his black slacks, and Leigh resented that "Kelsey, dear" was getting an eyeful of the thick pelt on Nick's wide chest. She clenched her fingers, resisting the urge to button his shirt and cover him from the other woman's gaze.

Nick gave Kelsey a bear hug and pulled her into the apartment. Leigh shut the door with a bang as she watched Kelsey place the sombrero on Nick's head and brush a kiss across his cheek. "He's trying to get the darn piñata out of my car."

"A piñata?" Nick asked with a chuckle.

Kelsey laughed. "You didn't think we'd go to Mexico without bringing you back something, did you? The sombrero is for you, but I couldn't resist the piñata. I thought you could give it to your nieces and nephews."

"The kids will love it. Have you met Leigh?" Nick turned to her, his eyes twinkling.

She scowled. Nick knew that jealousy was digging talons into her heart. He knew it and was enjoying it. Damn him! And damn her that she couldn't keep her feelings for him under control. Well, she didn't have to stay and watch this touching reunion.

"I'll leave you two alone," she muttered. The confusion in Kelsey's eyes and the unholy glee in Nick's eyes told Leigh she sounded rude. She forced herself to smile at the other woman. "I'm sure you and Nick have a lot to—"

A frantic tattoo pounded on the door, startling Leigh. The door pushed open under her hand, and a tall, thin man with a harried expression beneath his wire-rimmed glasses rushed in. He clutched a gigantic orange papier-mâché chicken. "For God's sake, let me in before someone sees me with this monstrosity," he said.

He sighed with relief as Nick took the Mexican toy and plopped it on the couch. "Yes, Dave. It wouldn't do for a CPA to be seen with anything as radical as an orange chicken."

Nick's teasing tone confused Leigh. Where did Dave fit into this? Their friendliness made it obvious they weren't rivals. But if they weren't, then—

Dave grinned. "You'd do the same. No man enjoys looking like a dork, walking through a public airport, toting something like that."

"You loved it," Kelsey said as she slipped her arm around his waist and gave him a hug. "You had every kid within sight following you around."

Dave's eyes were alight with indulgent humor as he returned her hug. "I'm afraid only you and Nick have the kind of nerve it takes to be a Pied Piper. You'll have to settle for me remaining the old stick-in-the-mud I am."

"I happen to love the dull, stodgy type," Kelsey said with a chuckle.

Watching them, Leigh felt a suspicion grow in her. "Nick, you never finished the introductions," she hinted.

Nick walked over and slipped his arm around her waist. She felt the heat mount in her cheeks as she noted the speculative gleam in Kelsey's expression.

"This is my secretary, Leigh Townsend. She lost power in the ice storm we had last week and has been staying here until it's restored."

Kelsey's expression immediately turned sympathetic and she approached Leigh, her hand outstretched. "God, how awful. It must be so frustrating to have your life disrupted like that. I'm Kelsey Huber and this is my husband, Dave."

Married? They're married! Leigh felt relief burgeon in her like a seedling in spring. She saw understanding in Kelsey's eyes as the other woman glanced from Leigh to Nick.

"It's so nice to meet you," Leigh said, putting all the warmth she could in her voice. Leigh liked the feel of Kelsey's firm handshake and her mellow, open friendliness. She sensed here was someone she could like and felt ashamed of her spiteful thoughts.

Dave swallowed her hand in his large bony one and smiled ruefully. "The storm is the reason we stopped by. I suspect the road to the house is a disaster. I figured we'd better pick up the Cherokee, so we can get to the house."

Leigh turned to Dave, surprised. "The Jeep belongs to you? I thought it was Nick's."

"No, it was still in the shop when we left, and Nick picked it up for me."

"Actually, the road's not too bad." Nick said as he removed a key from his key ring and handed it to the other man. "Leigh and I have been over it every day, feeding the horses, and the Jeep made it just fine." He tilted his head and grinned. "In fact, I think I just might have to get me one. I loved the way it goes over any terrain."

"Lord help us," Dave replied with a groan. "If you do, just don't let Kelsey talk you into cross-country racing with her. I have heart failure now, every time she takes off in the Pinto."

His wife poked him in the ribs. "You turkey. Just for that, I bet I beat you home."

"Kelsey..."

She flashed a smug smile at his warning, then blew a kiss to Nick as she sailed out the door. "See you later."

"Can't I offer you a drink before you leave?" Nick asked as he walked Dave to the door.

"No, thanks. I want to get home before dark." He nodded at Leigh. "Nice meeting you, Leigh. Have Nick bring you out to visit the horses anytime you want."

Nick turned after closing the door and leaned against it, his arms and legs crossed. Leigh's gaze trailed up from his bare feet—who would ever have imagined that naked feet could be sexy, she mused vaguely—along his powerful body to his rugged features. The very devil was in his expression, and all of a sudden Leigh was sure she didn't want to hear what was on his mind.

"What a charming couple," she said as she self-consciously fiddled with her belt. "Have they been married long?"

Nick pushed from the door with his shoulders and started toward her. "They met in fourth grade, and bam, it was love at first sight. There was never anyone else for either one."

"It's obvious they're soul mates." She stepped around the couch, her breath constricted as she watched his purposeful approach. If she didn't know better, she could think he was stalking her.

"Do I detect a note of envy, Leigh?"

Startled, she looked into his eyes, a shiver sliding up her spine at his expression. Laughter, tenderness and underlying it all, a fierce, burning hunger. His magnetic gaze seemed to reach straight into her brain, making it impossible for her to move her trembling legs. She stood, waiting, torn between the worry that he would kiss her and the anguish that he wouldn't.

He ran his finger over the exposed skin along the edge of her robe, down to the hidden cleft between her breasts. "What was the meaning of that scene with Kelsey?" he murmured, his gaze intent on his wandering digit.

"Wh-what do you mean?" Aware only of his searing path across her suddenly tight flesh, Leigh couldn't get any order to her thoughts.

"You all but announced to her we were lovers, Leigh."

With maddening determination, Nick continued his inexorable journey down the center of her body, circling her navel as he loosened the knot on her belt with the other hand until her robe opened. The cool air should have eased her uncomfortable warmth, but it didn't. If anything, the increasing heat robbed her of air, and when she felt Nick's palm curl around the curve of her stomach, she realized she'd stopped breathing. Her legs buckled and she grabbed Nick's shoulders. He fanned his fingers along her naked bottom, pulling her firmly against him.

"We'd better leave. We'll be late for our dinner reservations," she whispered. With desperation she sought her final chance to escape the erotic web he was weaving.

"Everything I'm hungry for is in this room."

His simple statement crumbled her last defense and she tilted her head back, searching for his mouth.

Nick felt her surrender and swept in, no quarter, no mercy. He laid his claim, his tongue darting in and out in mimicry of the action his loins screamed for. His heart pounded as he felt her nipples rasp against his chest and he ground the hardness between his thighs into her soft belly. "Sweetheart, you'd better not change your mind because I don't think I could stop," he growled.

"I won't."

In her gaze he could see everything he'd been hoping to see. Want, need...a blazing flame that matched his. "Then let me see what I've been imagining all this time." He slipped the wrap from her shoulders, marveling how the bright red color made her skin glow like fine ivory. The memory of a naughty angel tickled the back of his mind, but his body's demands let the thought drift away like mist.

She pulled at his shirt and he caught her hands, stilling her frantic movements. "No, we've waited too long. I intend to make it last—make it sweet and long."

"You once promised me hot and furious." She ran her tongue along her bottom lip, and a throb in his groin urged him to keep his promise.

"Then we'll do both. We'll start slow..." He ran his palms along her arms until he could cup her face. "And

AMANDA KRAMER

103

we'll finish hard and fast.'' He kissed her again, touching her only with lips and tongue and teeth. Her mouth, like all the dark mysteries of time, drew him to explore. He nibbled on the soft inner surface of her lower lip, then soothed it with a stroke of his tongue. Lord, he could feast for all eternity on just her mouth, but the scent of her, the sound of her whimpers were threatening his control.

Leigh felt a fine tremor in his hands and knew with certainty that the magic of that long-ago December night was about to be repeated. Only this time there was no haze to interfere with the clarity of her sensations. She leaned forward and dragged the tips of her nipples through his chest hair, catching her breath at the flood of arousal that stormed from her breasts to her body's center. She caught his groan in her mouth and chased it back with her tongue.

He gripped her hips and ground them into his. She laughed deep in her throat, pleased she had the power to excite him beyond madness. She pushed his shirt off his back, then dipped her hands beneath his waistband. She skimmed her fingers along his skin until she reached the front of his body and smiled into his startled eyes as he instinctively sucked in his abdomen. With a gentle hand, she proceeded to claim her prize.

''Leigh! Don't touch me or—''

''Stop me, then,'' she murmured as she curved her palm around his hardened shaft. The rasp of his zipper seemed to shatter his resistance, and he thrust forward as she took his arousal more firmly, caressing the rigid length until she could stroke the silky tip.

Wildfire roared through his head. ''You win,'' he said in husky tones and lifted her in his arms with fierce possession. ''Fast and furious.''

She looped her arms around his neck and nuzzled her soft cheek against his freshly shaved face. ''I prefer to think we both win.''

He stalked into the darkened bedroom and propped one knee on the bed as he laid her against the pillows. The light from the open door spilled across her body and cast her curves into shadow. A sense of the emotional and physical blended together and Nick felt completed. For a moment he knelt, frozen by the sight of her eyes, dark with Eve's allure. Then he forced himself off the bed and stripped off his slacks and briefs in one swift movement.

Her searing gaze on him made him understand how primitive man must have felt with his mate. The appreciative respect in her glance was enough to make him go from hard to rock hard. She held out her hand in entreaty, and he lay beside her, braced on an elbow. Fascinated, he watched her breasts rise and fall as she breathed in rapid pants. He traced his fingertips along the delicate blue veins around the dark, large aureole.

"How soft they are . . . firm and aroused. It's like a miracle to think what you will look like in a few short months, nurturing a new life." She tensed, and he glimpsed an eclipse of her desire before she veiled her eyes with her lids.

She clasped her hands behind his head and pulled him down to her. "Don't make me wait, Nick. I want you now."

She eagerly took his mouth. Even *now* he saw her as a mother? Well, he'd soon learn. Before she was through, he would see her as only a woman—all woman.

She reached between their bodies, and the power of his response drove all coherent thought from her mind. She'd wanted furious and that's what she got. A headlong plunge into the maelstrom. Like an ever-rising tide from a storm-ridden sea, his hands and lips stoked her passion to a frenzy. She heard her own whimpers and writhed uncontrollably under his body.

"Nick . . . oh, Nick. Please fill me," she moaned. "I can't wait."

His harsh gasps sounded in her ear. "Leigh . . . sweetheart. If I come in too fast, I might hurt you."

She gripped his hips, her nails digging into the knotted muscle. "I'm already hurting," she grated. "Now . . . please."

He entered her with one smooth thrust, then hesitated. She lightly bit his earlobe in frustration, and he began to move. She couldn't touch him enough . . . taste him enough. The pounding rhythm beat into her body, her heart . . . her very soul. She arched her hips, matching him thrust for thrust. The universe exploded like sheet lightning across the prairie, and she heard his triumphant cry before he collapsed in her arms.

Gulping for air, she felt his heartbeat match the hammering cadence of hers. He raised his head, his gaze intent on her, and she felt satisfaction at his dazed expression.

"That was incredible," he whispered, his heaving chest teasing her still-sensitive nipples. He brushed a dampened strand of hair from her cheek, then followed his fingers with his lips. "You are a fantastic lover, sweetheart."

She nuzzled her face against his throat, tender emotions spilling from her heart. Her throat too tight for words, she ran her hands over his sweat-slicked shoulders, trying to express all she was feeling with her touch.

He gave her a crooked grin. "Aren't you going to tell me how fantastic I was?"

She laughed, but replied obediently. "You were fantastic."

"And virile?"

"And virile."

"How about creative?"

She lightly slapped his hip. "You were fantastic, virile *and* creative. On a scale of one to ten, you come in with an eight point nine."

"What?"

"Now all we have to work on," she continued inexorably, "is your humility."

He nuzzled the tops of her breasts. "I'd rather work on the eight point nine. I'm sure with a little more practice I could get my score up to a perfect ten."

She gasped as his knee pinched the inside of her thigh and he immediately rolled off her to his side, his expression anxious. "I knew we should have gone slower. Is it the baby? Did we hurt him?"

Leigh closed her eyes in despair, gritting her teeth against the irritation. Damn, what did it take to get his mind off her pregnancy? She fought down her resentment. Okay, so he's concerned about the baby, she thought, struggling to be reasonable. He'd thought of her as a mother a lot longer than he'd thought of her as a lover. She would just have to be patient.

She gave him a quick kiss. "I'm fine…and so is the baby. All those books you got me say the baby is only about four inches long. He's floating in his own little world, safe from harm." A sudden yawn overwhelmed her and she nestled against his shoulder. "Now just hold me. I think I'm about to go to sleep on you."

His chuckle vibrated under her cheek. "Really?" he murmured as he wrapped her in his powerful arms and turned to his back, pulling her on top of him. "And I had such good ideas about making love slow and easy."

He caressed her spine with long, scorching strokes, and she felt him stirring between her legs. A slow heat built in her, driving out all traces of languor. She met his gaze, burning, questioning…promising.

She wiggled her hips in invitation. "Oh?" she whispered. "Show me."

Seven

———

Leigh lay spoon fashion behind Nick, his arm holding hers firmly to his waist even as he slept. A slow, easy rain trickled down the window, and the cold, lonely sound made her glad to be cozy in bed. Especially with Nick. She nestled closer to his strong back and inhaled deeply of his musky scent.

Her mind drifted back to the previous night. Just as he'd promised, they'd made love slow and easy, with a sensuality that melted her bones. Later, he'd awakened her with a midnight snack to cover the dinner they'd missed. Once their hunger for food had been satisfied, they had fallen back into bed to feed another hunger, one that had been months building. She wondered if her craving for him would ever be appeased and laughed quietly into the soft hair at the nape of his neck. Nick stirred, then turned onto his back, but didn't awaken.

She took the opportunity to explore his features. Thick black eyebrows winged over his closed eyes, fringed with long, dark lashes. With her fingertip, she lightly brushed along his rugged forehead, his cheekbones and his incredibly sensual full mouth, which drew her to kiss him with a butterfly touch. A faint smile crossed his lips, and he murmured something Leigh couldn't distinguish.

Leigh pulled back, a shard of fear piercing her heart. *Oh, God! Not again,* she prayed. Please don't let him call her Cara.

A small frown gathered between his brows. "Leigh?" he mumbled. "Sweetheart?"

Tears pricked in her eyes as she relaxed. She rolled forward slightly, resting her forehead against his temple. "Shhh. It's all right. I'm here," she whispered.

He grumbled in his sleep and rubbed his whisker-roughened face against her cheek. She lay still, afraid he'd awaken and see her distress. When his deepened breathing told her he had gone back to sleep, she sidled out of his arms and sat up on the edge of the bed.

In the gloomy morning light, she looked around Nick's bedroom, noticing details she was too involved to see the night before. The massive king-size bed with its brass headboard dominated the room. It was definitely a man's room with its traditional American oak furniture, and Leigh found she liked the forest green and burgundy colors. The central heat kicked in and she shivered as the air whispered across her skin. She rose, rubbing her arms, and tiptoed into the connecting bathroom. Closing the door, she found a dark blue silk robe hanging on a hook. She slipped into the wrapper, Nick's special scent rising from the soft folds. As she washed her face, she scrutinized her reflection in the mirror over the wash basin. She looked the most relaxed she had in weeks. She looked like a woman well loved and that's what she felt like. *But is it real or am I making another mistake?* she thought. Hadn't she felt the same about Brad?

The somber thought disturbed her, and she quietly left the bathroom. She paused a moment to stare at Nick. The sight of him, sprawled in the tumbled sheets like a sleek jungle cat, stirred an ache in her that had nothing to do with sex. She realized she wanted to hear his laughter, watch his expressive face as he talked about something that excited him. She wanted to share his thoughts and his dreams. She stood, frozen, unable to move as revelation struck her with the impact of a runaway train. God, she loved him.

She stumbled back against the door, shaking her head. *No!* She forced herself to take a deep breath. She had to remain calm. She glanced once more at Nick, then slipped out of the bedroom. *I can't be in love with Nick,* she told herself firmly as she walked through the living room. What she was feeling was just the aftermath of a night of lovemaking. Or maybe because she was carrying Nick's child, she was feeling an emotional connection that wasn't real. Whichever, she couldn't trust the feeling, and last night had probably been a mistake.

In the kitchen she started the coffeemaker and stared through the window over the sink while waiting for the coffee to brew. She wanted to regret last night, but she couldn't. It had been the most wonderful night of her life—exciting, passionate, full of fire and magic. And at the heart of it had been Nick.

Strange how four months ago, he'd been just her boss. A hunk, but eccentric. She'd always thought no one knew an employer like his secretary, but behind the image of the exacting lawyer, she'd found a man who intrigued her. Now... She sighed and shook her head. Now she didn't know what to think.

She sensed his presence a moment before he stepped behind her and slipped his arms around her waist.

"I missed you," Nick murmured. He nuzzled the side of her neck, and she instinctively leaned back against him. "Come back to bed. I can think of better ways to start the day than watching it rain."

She clamped down on her confused emotions and forced herself to chuckle. "I'll bet you can."

Conscious of the heat of his body along her back, her soft breasts cradled by his enclosing arms, she felt the banked-down embers from the night before fan to life within her. Alarmed, she realized he had the power to control her with a simple touch. *It's too soon,* she thought. She needed time to deal with feelings she'd been ignoring for too long. If she submitted to her need for him, her deep desire to feel him buried inside her, she'd be lost. Wouldn't she?

She turned in his arms. He wore only jeans, slung low on his hips, and she pressed her hands against his bare chest, the crisp hair tickling her palms.

"But if we're going to the flea market, we'd better get an early start." Amazed at how casual her voice sounded, especially when she thought her heart would pound its way out of her chest, she smiled at him. A strange expression crossed his face and Leigh imagined for a moment that somehow she'd disappointed him.

His mocking grimace made her doubt her impression as he shook his head.

"The woman has no mercy. You'd actually drag me out in this muck?"

She nodded, and he shrugged his shoulders.

"Okay, but you'd better make it worth my while not to go back to bed."

She stared at his sexy mouth, only inches away, his warm breath whispering across her lips. Helplessly she told herself she was crazy to even consider kissing him. But she couldn't help it. The thought of his taste, the feel of his hard chest against her aching breasts lured her like a lodestone. She pulled his mouth down to hers and shivered as his dark spell blurred the edges of her mind. She was having second thoughts about returning to bed when he broke the kiss.

"Very nice," he said with a wicked gleam in his eyes. "But what I had in mind was a cup of coffee."

Gratefully she recognized his attempt to keep the mood light. No doubt he was confused, wondering what was going on, but willing to follow her cues. His deference wouldn't last long, though... not if she knew Nick. Then what the hell would she tell him? That she might love him, but wasn't sure? Leigh felt a shiver crawl up her spine. No, she'd better wait until she had things worked out in her mind. Meanwhile she just had to keep things casual.

"I'm with you," she said, laughing as she slipped out of his arms and searched for two mugs in the cupboard. "Even if I still miss the caffeine." She set the mugs on the counter. "I sure hope I can get back into my house this weekend. I'm more than ready for my own territory."

Suddenly there were storm warnings in the air, and Leigh knew they had nothing to do with the weather outside.

Nick pulled her around to face him. "And what about last night? Was that just a one-night stand?"

Stunned, Leigh heard the echo of her own words from that long-ago night in December. She cupped his face in her hands. "Oh, no, Nick. Last night was special. You're the kind of lover every woman dreams of . . . tender, yet passionate. I've never felt more like a woman than I did in your arms. But . . ."

"But what, Leigh?"

She turned back to the coffee maker and poured out the dark brew. "I don't trust desire. Infatuation makes a very poor foundation for a relationship. Until I moved in here a week ago, we'd never even had a date."

He picked up his mug and leaned against the counter. "And you don't believe in love at first sight."

"First sight?" Leigh slanted a glance at him as she opened the refrigerator and took out a pitcher of orange juice. "We've known each other for over two years, Nick. That hardly counts as first sight."

"But you never really saw me as anything except a boss until last month, did you? And you certainly didn't think of me as a lover."

"Not exactly," Leigh said and sensed his sharpened interest.

"What does that mean?"

She felt heat mount her cheeks. Oh, Lord! How had she gotten into this conversation? "Well, you must know you've been the object of lascivious interest in the break room."

He shook his head and grinned. "Gossip. What did *you* think of me?"

"Uh . . . well, I guess . . ." she said as she shrugged her shoulders, keeping her gaze on the juice she was pouring. How did she tell him her erroneous image of him without sounding like a fool? She didn't, she decided with resignation. "I thought you looked sexy as hell, but were some kind of . . . of . . ."

"Don't stop now, Leigh."

His expression told her he wasn't going to let her off the hook. No wonder he was considered the best real estate lawyer in the state. He never gave up. "I thought you were some kind of stuffed shirt."

"You've called me that before. Based on what?"

She looked at him, irritated with his persistent questioning. "Based on little things such as refusing to have hamburgers delivered to the office."

"Smells up the office."

"Signing us up for those corporate challenges and then making us feel guilty if we didn't join, no matter the weather."

"Hey, it was for charity."

"And the way you stack up files in your office, then refuse to let me touch them."

"I know where everything is."

"But I don't and then you snarl at me when you call in for information from them and I have trouble finding the right file in that mess."

"But that way I can keep everything current right where I need it." He ran his hand through his hair at her derisive sniff. "Okay, okay, so you can put one of those file dividers on my desk. But no wild colors," he added with a scowl. "So far, all your complaints are superficial. What about the real me? Haven't you learned more about me than what I am in the office?"

She stopped closer and looped her arms around his neck. "Oh, yes, I have, Nick. I've learned you have a wicked sense of humor. You're generous, not only with your money, but with your time." She grinned at him. "And I learned you don't go to bed in a three-piece suit as has been suggested by certain parties."

He slipped his arms loosely around her waist, his hands stroking her hips. "Who said that?" he asked with a mock glare.

"Never mind. The point is I was wrong about what kind of man you are, but that doesn't mean I want to be involved with you."

"But you could?"

She stared at him, not trusting his bland tone. "Maybe. But only time will tell."

"You don't have time, Leigh. Soon you'll have a baby, a child who needs two parents to love him." He lightly gripped her chin with his fingers, his eyes almost black in his intensity. "That's why I think we should get married."

Leigh's mind froze, and she felt the fine hair on the back of her neck stir. Marriage? Nick had been thinking about marriage? Her heart thumped wildly at the idea, but at the same time she wanted to run. Her palms became damp when she realized how much she wanted to agree to his suggestion.

"No," she said, fighting to keep her voice firm. "We have no reason to get married."

"There's the baby."

Of course, she thought. The baby. Trust Nick to never lose sight of her pregnant state. "That's not good enough. There are almost more single parent families now than nuclear families. I don't need a husband just because I'm pregnant."

"We share a lot of interests."

"So, that makes us good friends, but it doesn't mean we should get married."

"We find each other sexy as hell." His voice was a low growl and she felt her nipples tighten in response.

"That's true," she said with a nervous laugh. "One touch from you and I can't think. All I want to do is wrap you around me."

"Is that so bad?" He reached for her and she stepped back, out of range.

"For me, it is. I don't trust my judgment anymore."

"And he didn't help any."

"He?"

Nick gestured toward her middle. "The guy who got you pregnant, then disappeared."

Good grief, Leigh thought. How could she forget Nick didn't know the truth about the baby? "He...he has nothing to do with this. Next month I get my bachelor's degree, and with luck, I'll start law school in September. Marriage would definitely interfere with my goals there."

"That's crazy, Leigh. Isn't your due date in September? How do you expect to start law school when you'll have a brand-new baby?"

Leigh felt as frustrated as he sounded. "I don't know. I'm still working things out in my mind." At his skeptical expression, Leigh plopped down in a chair at the kitchen table. "For God's sake, Nick, in this past month, I've found out I'm pregnant, had to leave my house, made love to the world's last living yuppie, and...and..."

Nick grinned at her as he refilled her mug before sitting in the chair opposite her. "And?"

"And I've got finals coming up." At the sound of the laughter rumbling out of him, she flashed him a rueful grin. "Okay, okay, so I've got six weeks before I have to worry about finals."

She looked down at her coffee, sorting through her jumbled emotions. "I feel as if I've lost control of my life, Nick. Three months ago, all my goals were lined up like ducks and I was picking them off, one by one. Now, no matter what I decide to do, I don't like the possible results. I want to have children, but not now. I want to share my life, my future with someone, but not yet. I'm not ready."

"Ready or not, you're going to have a child to provide for in about five months. Would it be so bad to give up law school, at least until the baby starts school? Another advantage to getting married is you could get rid of that wreck you live in."

Like a black hole, Leigh felt a region around her heart expand, sucking up all heat and light and sound. She rubbed her hands along her arms, but she couldn't warm the chill in her flesh. "So, to become a mother, all I have to do is quit school, sell my house and marry you. In other words, give up myself.''

Nick frowned. ''How does giving up your house mean you're losing yourself? I'd think you'd be glad to get out from under the expense, the hassles.''

Anger exploded in Leigh, melting the cold and dark with a white-hot flash. ''I didn't buy that house because I couldn't afford anything else. I bought it *because* it was a wreck, just like my life at that time. Rebuilding the house is the same to me as rebuilding my life, and I have no intention of giving up my dream.''

''Leigh—'' Nick reached for her, but Leigh evaded his hand, scraping her chair along the floor as she rose, her hands clenched.

''Don't touch me! Don't beguile me. One night in your bed, and you think it gives you the right to organize my life for me. You think I'll be so enthralled with your sexual prowess, I'll meekly go along with anything you say. My ex-husband cured me of that particular madness.''

''Enough!''

The fire in Nick's eyes warned Leigh, but she didn't care. She'd gone through this before, and she'd be damned if she'd do it again.

''No, not nearly enough. I'm immune to that kind of manipulation, Nick. You may be a hell of a lover, but you have no special power over me.''

''No?'' With two long strides, Nick was before her, his hands gripping her shoulders. ''Let's see just how immune you are to me, angel,'' he snarled.

His mouth sealed hers in a savage kiss. Leigh pummeled her fists against his hard-muscled stomach, but he moved closer, his arms sliding under hers to pull her tightly against him. His tongue's scalding demand for entry touched a chord within her traitorous body and Leigh heard herself moan in protest. Instantly Nick's mouth gentled as he coaxed, tempted her. Leigh tried to whip up her fading anger, but her senses reeled under his invasion. She felt his deft hands, strong and hard, on her breasts and she arched her back, instinctively demanding more.

Nick bent his head and tongued her nipple through the soft fabric of the robe. A sob clawed its way out of the back of her throat as she felt a shaft of pleasure-pain shoot through her body. Her knees buckled, and Nick eased her down to the carpeted floor, sweeping the robe off her shoulders.

She welcomed his weight as his mouth explored hers, every stroke of his tongue creating feverish peaks in her, each higher than the last. She whimpered in protest as he rolled off her and fumbled for his zipper. She clutched his arms and pulled him back to her, unwilling to lose contact with him for even as long as it would take for him to strip off his jeans. Relieved to feel his hard arousal settle in the cradle of her thighs, she ignored the tiny discomfort of the metal teeth scraping her inner thigh. Nick rocked against her, his hands and mouth stirring her desire until she was frantic for completion.

"Look at me, Leigh." Nick's harsh command called her and she opened her eyes, focused on his fierce stare. "Tell me to stop, Leigh. Tell me this is only a casual encounter for you, that you don't need this, and I'll stop."

She clasped his sweat-slicked shoulders. She fought to utter the words, but she *did* want him. And not just this moment, but for an eternity of loving and sharing. She wanted a lifetime of building a future with Nick, raising children and growing old together.

"Yes, Nick. I want you. Please . . ." Her words ended in a gasp as he thrust into her, filling her completely, totally. He pushed her, drove her to the precipice, and she cried out as they fell over the edge. She dissolved, lost to all time and space until the ecstasy ended, leaving her sobbing for breath in his arms. His tender mouth and loving hands eased her down until she lay in his arms, her face wet with perspiration.

He brushed her damp hair away from her face and skimmed his lips over her temple. "Don't tell me I don't have power over you, not when you respond to me the way you do."

She buried her face against his shoulder, shuddering as she realized he spoke the truth. "Is this where you convince me we get married and live happily ever after?"

He nudged her chin with his knuckle until she looked at him through tear-filled eyes. "No, because if you agreed, we'd both wonder if it *was* just the physical attraction between us. I'd feel like I was taking, and I don't want to take, Leigh. I want you to give...freely, without any doubts. That is the power you have over me."

She wanted to tell him she loved him. She wanted to tell him about the baby and about that long-ago December night. But she couldn't. These past few minutes had proved what she'd always feared. Nick only had to touch her, and her anger melted like mist before the sun. No, she couldn't trust her emotions; it could cost her too much. Once before she'd given all her trust and found betrayal. Now she wasn't even sure if she had any more trust in her.

"So where do we go from here?" she whispered.

He pulled the discarded blue robe over her as she lay cuddled against his side, lifted her hand and kissed her palm. "Damned if I know. A few minutes ago, I thought I had all the answers. We'd get married and raise the baby together. I never realized how driven you are to be independent."

She tilted her head so she could see him better. "Not just independent, Nick. If I get married again, I want to go in as an equal partner. I want my goals to be as important as his."

Nick frowned. "I'll be honest, Leigh. When I visualized a wife, it wasn't with a briefcase in her hand. I know in most marriages the wife has to work outside the home. But that wasn't what I wanted for my marriage. I believe in the traditional family, me making the living, my wife at home tending the hearth. I earn enough money that any wife of mine doesn't have to work unless she wants to. But then, I always thought I would marry someone who would want to stay home with the kids. None of the women in my family work, and to me that's the way it should be."

"That's what I've been trying to tell you. We don't share much, not enough to build a relationship on."

"We haven't had enough time to decide that, Leigh. At least we know each other's expectations. We can work from there. So, if you won't marry me, how would you feel about us living together?"

For an instant Leigh felt a twinge of pain at how easily Nick took her refusal. Appalled at her thoughts, she pushed away the hurt and tested his idea. Live together? Did he mean like sharing closets and shelf space and who-takes-out-the-trash today? Mornings and holidays and sick days? The warmth of his hand along her back scorched her skin, and instant images of long, passion-filled nights swept through her consciousness. Her nipples grew hard, and from his grin, she knew he'd noticed her response.

"Oh, Nick." She wrapped her arms around his neck and covered his face with kisses. "Every time I think I have you pegged, you surprise me."

"Does this mean you agree?"

"No, but I love you for making the offer. You'd really be willing to go against everything you believe in, just for me?"

He nuzzled his chin against her hair. "I'm not being no-ble. After last night my desire for you has turned into a raging need. I told you I wanted you to give yourself freely to me and if it is only as a lover, then I'll take that." He tilted his head so he looked into her eyes. "Or were you thinking we could ignore last night?"

"My brain tells me to say yes," she said wryly. "But my body doesn't agree. I know that once having made love with you, I won't be able to keep my hands off you."

"Okay. Then as of now, we're officially lovers, but we each keep our own place."

She eyed him cautiously. Was it going to be that easy? No impassioned pleas about marriage? No more arguments about her incomplete house? About law school?

He smiled and drew her head down to his chest. "Don't look so suspicious, Leigh. Everything will work out. Just wait and see."

She nestled against him, content for now not to worry. After a few moments she felt Nick's chest vibrating under her cheek as he chuckled. She raised her head and saw the rueful smile on his face.

"What?" she asked.

"I've never made love on a floor before. You're a bad influence on me, Ms. Townsend."

"I've always said you needed more spontaneity in your life."

"I must say, now that I've indulged, it's not half bad. We'll have to do this again."

"Easy for you to say," Leigh retorted, rubbing her hand along her stinging backside. "You're not the one with rug burn."

Nick peered over her shoulder. "Poor baby. Want me to kiss it and make it better?"

"Gee, would you?"

"Sure, but that might lead to increasing your burn."

Leigh felt heat rise in her face, and Nick laughed again. He rose to his feet, pulling her with him. With his hands spanning her waist, he turned her and gently shoved her toward the bedroom. "Go get dressed while I cook breakfast. We'll call your neighbors and see if your house has electricity yet. If not, we'll go to the flea market. Hey . . ."

Leigh paused in the doorway and looked at him over her shoulder. He had tugged up his jeans, but hadn't fastened them. Helplessly her gaze followed the mat of dark hair as it traveled down his chest and temptingly disappeared in the vee of his opened zipper. She moistened her dry lips and forced herself to meet his knowing smile. "What?"

"You have a star on your hip," he said as he ambled over to her and stroked his finger over the discoloration at the top of her hip.

She glanced down, thrilling to his touch. "It's a birthmark."

"I like it. Makes me think I have my own Christmas star."

Leigh drew in her breath sharply. Was he starting to remember?

Nick frowned. "Strange. I feel like I've said that before, but I know this is the first time I've seen your birthmark." He shook his head as he laughed. "Must be that déjà vu again."

For a poignant moment, she felt hurt that he still had no recollection of a night that haunted her. Then she caught herself. What was wrong with her? What would she do if he did remember the party? If he remembered that when they'd made love, he'd kissed her birthmark, murmuring about his private Christmas star? She shuddered at the idea.

"What's wrong, Leigh?"

"Wrong?" She was having trouble hearing him. Every time he mentioned Christmas, guilt gripped her heart.

"Nothing's wrong, Nick," she lied as she forced herself to smile. "Sometimes you just startle me when I hear you saying something so romantic. Nobody at the office would believe me if I told them you thought of my birthmark as a Christmas star."

He brushed a kiss across her lips. "Don't look at me like that or we'll never get out of here today."

He nudged her toward the bedroom again and ambled to the refrigerator. Leigh fled from the kitchen, her heart pounding. As she stood in the shower under the steady beat of the water, she wondered if she hadn't made a mistake by getting more involved with Nick. How was she supposed to keep her secret if they were lovers? Her heart told her she should tell him everything, but her head told her that would be a tactical error. She sighed and raised her face, wishing the water would wash away her lies as easily as it rinsed the shampoo from her hair. Why couldn't she follow her heart when it came to Nick?

"From the expression on your face, you'd think that piece of junk was a treasure."

Nick looked up from the massive old rocking chair he'd been examining and grinned at Leigh. "By the time I get through, this chair will look like a family heirloom." He took a moment to appreciate the picture she made as she stood in the doorway of her spare room with a steaming mug in her hands.

The light gleamed in her disordered curls, still damp from the rain. She'd changed from her wet clothing, and Nick felt a stab of desire despite the fact the form-fitting T-shirt illustrated her fuller breasts, her thickening waist, all the changes pregnancy was making in her figure. He ran his gaze down her body and felt his lips twitch at the sight of the black tights that covered her legs.

She glanced down, then flushed. "I don't have any clean jeans left. At least, none I can fasten anymore. I really need to break down and buy some maternity clothes."

He laughed as he rose from his squatting position. "I kind of like it. It makes you look wild and sexy." He chuckled as her blush deepened.

She handed him a mug. "I don't know how you can call this Irish coffee when it's made with decaf, but I thought you'd be ready for something warm." As welcome as the rich smell of hot coffee and whiskey was, he loved her warm woman scent more.

He took a sip, then gestured toward the rocking chair. "What do you think? Looks good in here, doesn't it?"

With a doubtful expression, she eyed the battered rocker. "Whatever possessed you to buy this thing? The headpiece has a large crack down the middle, and the back is missing three spindles."

Nick promptly sat in the chair and started rocking. "But the seat is sound and the rocking is smooth." He held out his hand. "Come here and let's try it out."

Leigh walked toward him slowly. "I doubt it will hold us both."

"Sure it will." Nick placed his mug on the floor, then patted his lap. "Come on. Trust me."

Leigh carefully lowered herself to Nick's knees, her body tense.

"Relax. It won't collapse." He pulled her against his chest and turned her so she lay across his lap with her head nestled on his shoulder. "Now, isn't this comfortable? They don't make rocking chairs like they used to."

Leigh settled against him and curled her arm around his neck. "I still think you paid the guy at the flea market way too much for this thing. For the same money, you could have bought a new one."

Nick stroked along her leg and felt her body melt against his. "But this one has tradition," he murmured into her soft, fragrant hair. "It's held generations of mothers with their children. I can see you, rocking your baby, breast-feeding him."

Leigh raised her head and stared at him. "You bought the rocker for me?"

"Sure. Every nursery needs a good rocking chair."

Leigh's startled expression clouded over. "I...I won't have a nursery. I've decided to give the baby up for adoption."

Pain slammed through Nick's chest, and he wondered if it could have hurt more if she'd punched him in the stomach. "Why, Leigh?" He had to force the words past his tight throat.

She looked away from him. "Adoption is the best thing for the baby. Law school takes a lot of time, time I wouldn't have to be a mother. The baby deserves better than to have someone who is either always working or studying."

"And God forbid anyone should interfere in Leigh Townsend's destiny, right, sweetheart?"

Leigh stiffened at his harsh words. She pushed herself off his lap. "Damn you, Nick! I'm not talking about dumping the baby into an orphanage. I've already talked this over with my doctor, and he has some patients he says would make wonderful adoptive parents."

"That certainly clears up all the untidy ends, doesn't it?" He rose, and the harsh light from the bare ceiling bulb showed the uncompromising line of his clenched jaw. His dark stare bore into her eyes with a fierce scowl, and Leigh faced him, refusing to be intimidated by his anger.

"One bad marriage, wham..." he said as he snapped his fingers. "Give up on marriage. Never mind that you were young and made a mistake. Get involved with a jerk who turns out to be married," again he snapped his fingers.

"Give up on passion. Never mind the creep thinks with his gonads."

"I... I'm just trying to do what's best for the baby. I—"

"If you surrender the baby for adoption," he said, ignoring her words, "you won't have to worry that you may get overwhelmed by motherhood. Your precious individuality would be safe, wouldn't it, Leigh?" He realized his tone was abrasive, condemning, but damn it, how could she even *think* about giving away her baby?

She opened her mouth and then paused, her expression changing from anger to wonder. She flattened her hand on her abdomen, her eyes wide.

"What is it? What's wrong?" Remorse swept away his anger. What was the matter with him? Didn't he know better than to upset a pregnant woman? And especially Leigh, when he knew how fragile she felt?

"He moved," she said. "I think I felt him move."

Nick grinned at the wonder of her tone and slipped his hand under hers, putting his other arm lightly around her waist. "I can't feel anything. This is one moment that only you can share with him." He was amazed at how disappointed he felt.

She tapped her first two fingers on the back of his hand. "He feels like that, like a tiny ripple. It's almost as if he's knocking."

Nick was silent for a moment, envious that he couldn't share the experience. "You know, this is the first time you've referred to the baby as 'him' rather than 'it.' Maybe he's trying to get into your heart."

Leigh's gaze met his. The vulnerability in her expression twisted his stomach. She shuddered, and Nick sat in the rocking chair, pulling her into his lap.

"It's the first time your pregnancy's been real to you, isn't it, Leigh?" he whispered as he drew her head down to his shoulder.

She nodded. "Sounds stupid, doesn't it? I mean, I've changed my whole life-style. I've given up cigarettes and junk food, had two months of morning sickness, but until this moment, he wasn't real. I don't know what I expected. Maybe I thought I was some kind of surrogate mother, growing a baby for some other woman. Or maybe I thought he would just kind of hang around in there until I was ready to be a mother. But now I realize I have another life inside me. Another being who has needs and demands, a person who will have his own dreams and triumphs.''

"How do you feel about that?"

Leigh sighed. "Scared . . . worried . . . confused . . ."

"Trapped?"

"I'm not sure. I did when I first found out I was pregnant. I *should* feel trapped. I mean, I had my whole life planned, and nothing is going the way I want. Oh, Nick, when did I lose control?"

"You haven't lost control, honey. Life changes on us, but control means we adapt to those changes." He nudged her chin, tilting her face toward him. "I'm betting on you, Leigh. You'll find your answers and later wonder why you ever doubted which way to go."

"I already have my answers," she said, her voice wavering. "The baby moving changes nothing. I'm still going to give him up for adoption."

Nick forced himself not to smile at her tone. She sounded like a kid whistling in a dark graveyard. He brushed his lips across the frown marring her brow, then pushed her head back to his shoulder.

"Shh, sweetheart. You'll get no more arguments from me. Just relax and let me hold you both for a while."

Time seemed to expand around them as he slowly rocked, savoring the pressure of her soft breasts pressed against his chest. A cold, lonely rain trickled down the window, and the feel of Leigh, warm and trusting in his arms, made him realize how protective he felt toward her.

As Leigh relaxed more against him, he silently cursed her ex-husband. If that bastard hadn't stripped Leigh of everything, she wouldn't be afraid to love again, especially her own child. Well, he'd be damned if he'd let Brad Townsend win. Between him and the baby, Leigh would learn love wouldn't diminish her. If he had anything to say about it, Leigh was going to find out that love would make her more than she ever hoped to be.

Eight

Leigh halted as she stepped into her office, then flinched as Nick bumped her from behind.

"What the—" Nick muttered over her shoulder and Leigh silently echoed the sentiment. To say the office was in an uproar was an understatement, she thought. The computer printer clattered off reams of paper, and the other line on Leigh's phone jangled even as a harried Maggie talked into the receiver. Leigh could see the late-May sunlight pour in the window behind Connie as she scribbled madly at Nick's desk while using the phone. In the corner the copier cranked along, filling the air with the sharp smell of toner.

"Give me those figures again, please." Maggie glanced up, then waved them in before entering figures into a laptop keyboard.

Leigh swiftly walked around the desk and peered at the tiny monitor. "It's the Morrison property," she told Nick as he approached the desk. "It looks like the consortium in

Oregon is ready for some serious talking about the industrial park.''

Maggie nodded without ceasing her work and Nick grinned. ''Great. This could be the biggest deal the firm's handled yet.''

Connie left Nick's office, flipping pages on her steno pad. ''Boy, am I glad to see you, Mr. Romano. Mr. Quint called to see if you could meet with them tomorrow morning. Mr. Kiefer told him you'd be there.'' She referred to her notes. ''I've got you booked in at the hotel, and a rental car will be available for you at the airport. I'm still waiting for flight confirmation, but it looks like we'll be able to get you out on the six o'clock flight tonight. That will give you a good night's sleep before the meeting at nine.''

Leigh swallowed a rising giggle when she saw the look of amazement on Nick's face. Connie wasn't anything like the klutz she'd been two months ago, and Leigh felt pride swell inside her when she saw how confidently her protégé listed what she'd done. Leigh knew training Connie as her replacement during her maternity leave had been a smart move.

''Good work, Connie. Now all we have to do is update the presentation material.'' Leigh tossed her purse on the desk.

Connie smiled and tore off the stream of paper from the now silent printer. ''Already done. Once the typing pool completes this last bit, I'll finish the brochure.'' An expression of apprehension crossed her face as she gathered the computer sheets into a neat pile. ''I . . . I hope no one minds, but I found some beautiful conceptual sketches in the file and I thought . . . well, maybe we could add them. You know . . . kind of give them a visual idea of the possibilities for the place.''

Leigh exchanged a grin with Nick, then he laughed and gave a thumbs-up sign. ''Damn, we're good.''

Connie blushed and scurried out of the office.

Maggie hung up the phone and slumped down in the chair, shoving her pencil into the tousled hair over her ear.

"You two may be used to this hectic pace, but I'm getting too old to rush around like this."

"You know you love it." Nick walked around the desk and bent over to kiss her lightly on the cheek. He picked up her notes. "Now, what's left to do?"

"Doris is waiting for those figures. Once she gets them typed in, Connie's going to run everything down to the print shop for a full-color job. All you have to do is pack a suitcase and make your flight."

"Great. I'll take this to Doris. Then I need to fill Drew in on what to cover for me over the next few days." He halted at the door and winked at Leigh. "Show Maggie our first picture of Sweetpea, honey."

Leigh stared after him, disturbed by a vague thought. Sure, she'd being training Connie to take over while she was off from work, but somehow, she'd never realized how much she was used to being a team with Nick. The idea that she wasn't indispensable was...disconcerting. She shook her head. What a stupid thought. Hadn't she been worried, just a few months ago, that part of Nick's attraction to her was her value in the office?

"Yoo-hoo. Earth calling Leigh. Are you there, Leigh?"

Maggie's voice cut through Leigh's thoughts, and she looked at the older woman's amused expression. Maggie cocked an eyebrow. "Sweetpea?"

Leigh chuckled. "Ever since we saw a rerun of *Popeye* on cable a couple of nights ago, Nick's been calling the baby Sweetpea. He fell in love with the baby in the movie." She dug through her purse until she found a small manila folder, removed a six-inch piece of X-ray film, and handed it to Maggie. "That's what Nick calls the baby's first picture. I had my sonogram today."

"Sonogram?" Maggie looked up from her perusal of the blurred image, a concerned expression wrinkling her brow. "They don't do sonograms unless there's something wrong."

"Nothing's wrong, Maggie. Nowadays, they do sonograms routinely." Leigh chuckled as she leaned against the corner of the desk and gestured to the film. "Nick was hoping that would show us which sex we had, but the technician said the baby had his legs crossed and she couldn't tell for sure."

"Which sex *we* had?" Maggie eyed her with speculation. "Does that mean you've decided to tell Nick the truth about the baby?"

"No," she mumbled. The old familiar panic and guilt tightened her throat. She knew she had to tell Nick, but once she did, would her life ever be her own again?

Maggie slapped her hands on the desk and Leigh flinched.

"For God's sake, Leigh. What's holding you up? You and Nick have been lovers for two months. Surely if you trust him with your body, you can trust him with the truth."

"Maggie!" Leigh felt heat rise in her face at her friend's blunt statement. "It's not that simple." She wandered to the window, leaned against the wall and stared unseeing at the traffic in the street below. "You don't understand. Sometimes when I see how much I've changed in these past few months, it scares me. I'll be shopping and find myself reading labels to find if it has too much sodium. Thursday..." She turned to face the older woman and crossed her arms across her breasts. "Thursday I felt guilty because I went to McDonalds for a hamburger and fries. And it makes me wonder how much of the change is because of what I feel for Nick."

"In some ways, you have changed."

Leigh quirked the corner of her mouth in cynical amusement. "You're not helping here much, Maggie. The thing I fear most is changing."

Maggie was silent for a moment. "Did you ever think that maybe you're finally shedding the emotional baggage left over from your marriage? When I first met you, there were only three things in your life—school, your job and that damned house. You looked for ways to avoid becoming involved with people."

"That's not true." Leigh flung out a hand in protest. "I did other things."

Maggie whirled her forefinger in a small circle.
"Whoopee. You went to the movies once every three
months and made a birthday party now and then. Big deal.
You dodged showers, bridal and baby, like they were the
plague. And if any activity had real live males, that was almost a guarantee you wouldn't be present."

"You make it sound as if I avoided men."

"Didn't you?"

"Don't be absurd. I dated, didn't I?"

Maggie scoffed. "Dweebs. And you usually only dated
them once. Since you and Nick have become an item, you
actually look like you're living. Personally, I think you owe
a lot to Nick. He's dragged you, kicking and screaming,
back into the human race. I'll bet you're more like the
woman you would have been if you hadn't married that
jerk who stole your self-confidence."

Leigh hated to admit it, but Maggie was right. She had
been living like a hermit since the divorce.

She lifted her hands in surrender and laughed. "Okay,
okay. I believe you. I've changed and for the better. But
there are other problems, things you—"

"Leigh, bring your pad," Nick ordered as he strode
through the doorway. "And Maggie, if you're finished
here, Drew wants you back at your desk."

He went into his office. Through the open door, Leigh
watched him grab the phone and punch in numbers. She
exchanged a wry smile with Maggie, then the older woman
collected her equipment. As Maggie headed around the
desk, she halted and placed her free hand on Leigh's arm.

"If you and Nick have problems, then work them out
together." She grinned, and Leigh sensed Maggie's confi-
dence in her. "After all, you and Nick are a hell of a team
here. Why shouldn't you be the same outside the office?"

"Leigh!"

Maggie grimaced. "I'd better go or we'll hear Drew
yelling, too."

Leigh laughed, picked up her pad and pencil and walked
into Nick's office, closing the door behind her. "You bel-

lowed, master?'' she teased as she seated herself and opened her pad.

Nick flashed a grin and continued sorting through his files. ''Reschedule all my appointments for the rest of the week except the Thompson meeting. Drew will take that one. Then dig out Masterson's file. He says he can fit me in if I can get there before four.''

''What about your speech at the Rotary Club?''

''Drew's doing it. And he'll go to the chamber of commerce breakfast tomorrow. Now, let's clear the rest of my letters.'' His phone rang and he picked up the receiver. ''Romano.''

Leigh tucked the folders he gave her into his briefcase as he listened to the person at the other end.

''I appreciate your hard work, but there is no way I can make that flight,'' he said, his gaze on Leigh. ''I have a graduation to attend. Have you got anything later?''

Leigh stared at him, startled.

''Three thirty-five is fine. Book a first class seat for Nick Romano... Yes, I'll be there an hour before the flight. Thank you.'' Nick hung up the phone, walked around the desk and slipped his arms loosely around her waist. ''Close your mouth, Leigh, or you'll catch flies. On second thought, don't.''

She accepted the hard, warm crush of his mouth and shivered as desire trickled from his sweetly probing tongue through the center of her body. She forgot they were in an office where anyone could walk in at any moment. She forgot the letters, the calls, even the urgency to get Nick caught up enough to leave town. All she could think about was the magic of his kiss... and how much she was going to miss him.

''Did you think I would forget your graduation, honey?'' he whispered, his breath stirring the hair at her temple. ''You worked long and hard to get this degree and I intend to be there tonight to see you get it. I'm proud of you.''

''But, you hate red-eye flights. You won't get any sleep and—''

"I wouldn't get any sleep without you next to me anyway. Do you realize this will be the first time we've been separated?"

Nick slipped his hands under the hem of her maternity top. The heat of his palms scorched her skin as he stroked up her spine. Her breasts felt tight and heavy nestled against his broad chest. She snuggled into him and slid her hands behind his neck, her fingers tangled in the thick, dark hair at his nape. Nuzzling the side of his neck, his taste burst rich and virile on her tongue, his scent musky, male to her senses. The strength of his arms around her made her feel protected, cherished, and she ached for... Lost in the magic of her body's demands, Leigh couldn't identify the hunger swirling through her.

Nick groaned deep in his throat and his arms tightened, drawing her even closer to him. As he pulled her rounded abdomen against him, the baby kicked, and Nick laughed softly.

"Oh, *cara,* I'm going to miss you both so much."

Pain rippled through Leigh's heart. Cara? Again? She fought free of his arms and stood facing him, clenched hands on her hips. "Who the hell is Cara?"

"What?" Confusion and desire warred in Nick's expression.

"One night, in your sleep, you called me Cara. Now I want to know who she is."

Nick looked at her, a gentle smile on his face. "My grandfather once told me that the minute he saw my grandmother, he knew he was going to marry her. From then on she was *cara* to him. That's Italian for *beloved one.*"

He lifted his hand and stroked the back of his fingers along her cheek. Leigh saw the tenderness in his eyes and felt herself melt under its warmth.

"Sometimes," he whispered as he continued his gentle caress, "when my heart is full of you, that is what I call you in my mind."

Tears pricked in Leigh's eyes and she swallowed the hard lump in her throat. All these months she'd been worried that she was some kind of substitute for Nick, and here he was, telling her he'd been holding her like a secret treasure in his mind since December. Somehow, his simple confession flowed through her like a balmy spring breeze. What was she going to do with this man? Every time she thought she had him pegged, he said something that threw her totally off balance. He was so open . . . so honest. Could she be any less? She had to tell him the truth.

"Nick . . ." She took a deep breath, trying to gather her courage. "I have something to—"

A sharp rap tore into the intimate moment, and Leigh glared at the closed door, wishing bad things to the person who had interrupted.

Nick laughed and dropped a quick kiss on her lips. "Don't worry. We'll finish this later." He stepped away from her and turned to face the door. "Come in."

Connie entered, her arms full of papers. "Wait until you see the great job the printer did." She laid the stack on Nick's desk and handed a booklet to him.

Leigh watched as he looked through the colorful brochure, but her thoughts were far from focused in a mere business deal. Had she been out of her mind? Okay, yes, she had to tell Nick the truth about the baby, but it wasn't something she could just blurt out. And when she did tell him... She shuddered at the thought. No, what she needed was to find the right time, sometime when they could sit and talk calmly. Sometime when she didn't have to worry about graduation and he wasn't pushing to make a flight. But no matter what, she would have to tell him.

"Leigh?"

She looked up and saw him holding out the booklet. She took it and forced herself to look at the pages. Oh yes, she would have to tell him . . . and soon.

Leigh pulled an envelope from the computer printer and clipped it to the appropriate letter. Walking into Nick's office, she placed both on the stack of correspondence ready for his signature. She checked to see everything was ready for his homecoming, then sat in the desk chair. She swiveled to face the window and snuggled in the comforting softness of the massive seat. The rich aroma of leather mingled with the special scent that reminded Leigh of Nick, and she felt her breasts tighten. How had she ever made it through the long days and even longer, lonelier nights?

Nick's trip to Oregon, expected to last three days, had dragged out for eight interminable ones. She would never have believed she could have missed him so much. When she got him alone, she would—

The sound of footsteps in her office interrupted her thoughts, and she whirled the chair around, her heart pounding in her chest. Maggie entered, carrying a blooming azalea plant, and Leigh slumped as disappointment flooded her.

"What a face," Maggie teased as she placed the flower on the desk. She glanced at her watch. "His plane landed about twenty minutes ago, and if I know Nick, he collected his luggage within ten. So with luck, he should be here anytime."

Leigh laughed and lightly touched the pale pink petals, their scent delicate in the air. "What's this?"

"Oh, just a little present from Nick."

"For me?"

"He certainly didn't send them to me."

Her heart pounding with excitement, Leigh snatched up the small card. She smiled as she read his simple message: "My road to home is you. Love, Nick."

Maggie flopped down in the client's chair. "I know I don't have to ask if you're glad he's coming home."

"Is it that obvious?"

Maggie quirked her lips. "Oh, no. Other than the fact that this is the first time all week you haven't been moping around with your lower lip dragging on the ground."

Leigh looked away from the older woman's knowing smile, feeling heat inundate her face. "At one time, if anyone had told me I would miss Nick Romano, I would have called them crazy."

"But you do."

Leigh sighed. "Oh, yes. Considering that I don't even live with the man, it's amazing what a hole he leaves in my life when he's gone. I miss the sound of his off-key singing in the shower. I miss the sight of him working in the kitchen, wearing his stupid Kiss the Cook apron. I even miss him barking out orders like some damn Marine drill instructor."

"Boy, you've got it bad, Leigh." Maggie hesitated, making aimless circles with her forefinger on the arm of the chair. "So, have you thought any more about telling him the truth about the baby?"

Leigh wasn't fooled by Maggie's casual question. "I hope I have a better idea." She pulled a small jeweler's box from her pocket and opened it, displaying a man's gold ring set with a gray cat's-eye stone. "I picked this up today. What do you think?"

Maggie whistled softly in appreciation. "It's gorgeous. Nick should love it."

"Enough to accept it as an engagement ring?" Leigh chuckled when Maggie widened her eyes. "I know it sounds weird, but I want Nick to understand how much I really trust him. Not with just the baby, but with my life, too."

Maggie grinned. "I think it's a great idea. So how are you going to do it?"

Leigh snapped closed the box and slipped it back into her pocket. "I've made arrangements at the Atlantic Sea Grill for tomorrow night."

"Wow, his favorite restaurant. But are you sure you want to tell him about the baby in such a public place?"

Leigh smiled with wry amusement. "We both know Nick doesn't do it often, but when he loses his temper…well, I'd just as soon not go through it. I'm hoping a lot of people around will keep Nick from killing me."

"Honey, if you believe that, you're kidding yourself."

Maggie's solemn expression touched an echo in Leigh's breast. "I'm not as flippant about telling Nick as I appear. I know he's going to be furious, and frankly I wouldn't blame him. I should have told him from the beginning."

She stroked a velvety azalea petal, forcing down her impending sense of disaster, before meeting Maggie's concerned stare. "But I'm counting on his love to help get him beyond the anger. I'm also hoping he will be so thrilled to finally have a child, one of his own, that he'll understand why I didn't tell him as soon as I knew."

"Maybe he'll be too excited to get angry."

Maggie didn't appear to believe her own statement, and Leigh grimaced. "And maybe if I feed him enough lobster, he'll be too full to yell. My mother always told me to feed a man before you tell him something you know will upset him."

"Ain't that the truth," Maggie drawled. "Well, I wish you luck." She glanced at her watch. "How about a break?" The phone rang and she frowned. "Why is it the phone always rings when you're dying for a cup of coffee?"

Leigh laughed as she picked up the receiver. "Hold on. This will probably only take a minute. Mr. Romano's office."

"May I speak to Ms. Townsend, please?"

"Speaking." Leigh frowned, trying to identify the male voice.

"Ms. Townsend, I'm Dr. Porter, dean of the University of Tulsa Law School."

Leigh caught her breath. He had to be calling about her application. "Dr. Porter."

"Ms. Townsend, our admissions board will start meeting with candidates next week for interviews, and I'm calling to encourage you to withdraw your application."

"Withdraw? Why?"

"I had lunch with your boss the other day and he told me about your pregnancy. As you know, competition for law school is fierce and . . ."

Leigh heard the dean talking about grade points and testing scores, but her mind whirred as if out of gear. Somewhere inside her, pain waited to erupt, and she gripped the phone tightly, determined not to cry. *Nick had betrayed her.* The dull ache in her turned into seething fury.

Damn him. It was all she could do to keep from screaming.

"My boss told you about my pregnancy, did he?" she said, cutting through the dean's monologue. She ignored Maggie's frantic motions of denial. "How conscientious of him."

"Actually, it kind of slipped out."

"I'll bet it did," Leigh muttered.

"What was that, Ms. Townsend?"

"Nothing, Dr. Porter. You know, of course, you can't legally deny me admission because of pregnancy."

Dr. Porter chuckled dryly. "Of course not, Ms. Townsend. Your file is impressive and I have little doubt you would be accepted."

The sincerity in his voice eased some of Leigh's anger.

"However," he continued, "if you had to drop out due to lost class time, it might be more difficult to reenter. I would recommend you withdraw and reapply for the next class."

Leigh squeezed her eyes shut. She needed to make a decision, but all she could think about was how Nick was up to his old tricks. Just when she thought he had learned not to interfere in her life, he pulled a stunt like this.

"I'll need some time to think things over, Dr. Porter. I'll call you with my decision first thing Monday morning."

"I understand, Ms. Townsend." He hesitated. "Give that scoundrel you work for my greetings. He was one of my students, and there are quite a few stories I could tell you about him."

"I'll bet you could." She understood Dr. Porter was trying to ease the tension, but she was in no mood to give Nick a break. "I'll tell that...scoundrel everything he needs to hear. And thank you for calling."

Leigh replaced the receiver and braced her elbows on the desk, rubbing her forehead with her fingertips. "That was the dean at U.T. He suggests that I reconsider my application to law school."

"Oh, honey." Maggie patted Leigh's hand. "I'm so sorry."

"At least they were impressed enough to call me personally. What makes me angry is how Nick stabbed me in the back."

"Nick wouldn't do that."

"Oh, really? I can just imagine what happened. Nick probably saw Dr. Porter at the alumni luncheon he went to a couple of weeks ago. No doubt the dean asked him for a personal evaluation. After all, I listed Nick as a reference, didn't I?"

Leigh stood and slowly paced, her arms folded beneath her breasts. "It was just one old buddy talking to another, right? I can hear Nick now. 'Yes, Ms. Townsend is a good candidate, but...oh, didn't you know? Ms. Townsend's pregnant. In fact, the baby's due mid-September, so she'll probably miss a couple months of classes.'"

Maggie shook her head. "Nick wouldn't deliberately sabotage your plans."

"Wouldn't he? Nick's never hidden the fact he doesn't approve of me going to law school."

"I think he's more concerned about the adoption. You know he feels that you wouldn't be giving the baby up if you weren't so obsessed with school."

"The adoption?" Stunned, Leigh sank into the chair opposite Maggie. She placed her hand protectively over her rounded abdomen. Give away Sweetpea? For an instant a fierce protective anger surged through her. Never! As if in affirmation, she felt the baby move inside her. "There isn't going to be any adoption."

"I'd already figured that out. After all, you were hardly thinking of marrying Nick and still giving the baby away. Just out of curiosity, when did you decide?" Maggie asked with a grin.

Leigh sighed, her lips trembling. "I'm not sure." She blinked back tears. "That's not true. I think I've known ever since the first moment I felt the baby moving. I just never admitted it, even to myself."

"Then you can't blame Nick for thinking you are still considering adoption. All he knows is that you won't marry him. He still thinks you're planning to place the baby and go to law school.''

Leigh frowned. "Yes, but that doesn't mean he should have gone behind my back and told Dr. Porter about my pregnancy.''

"Now, Leigh, don't jump to conclusions. Talk to Nick first.''

Maggie's right, Leigh thought. After all, hadn't she been wrong about "Cara,'' spent months worrying that Nick was in love with someone?

"All right, but I *am* going to ask him about his little chat with Dr. Porter.''

"And your plans for tonight?''

"We'll see how it goes.''

Suddenly the door opened and Nick was there. His gaze locked on Leigh's and she felt his lure. He's home, she thought, and she automatically moved toward him, then stopped. How could her body dare want him when he was such a rat?

Maggie glanced at Leigh and grimaced. "I believe this is my cue to leave,'' Maggie murmured as she sidled around them. "Welcome back, Nick.''

"Thanks, Maggie. It feels good to be home.'' He placed his briefcase on the desk and watched Maggie leave before turning to confront Leigh. He cupped her face in his hands. "Oh, angel, I've missed you . . .''

She pulled her face from his grasp and stepped back, putting the client's chair between them.

"Leigh?''

"I got a call from Dr. Porter just now.''

"From U.T.?''

She noted his wary expression and the hair at her nape stirred. "Yes, he called to recommend that I withdraw my application to law school.''

Nick frowned. "I don't understand. Why would he want you to withdraw?''

"Because of my pregnancy.''

He widened his eyes. "They can't refuse you because you're pregnant.''

Was there a spark of satisfaction in his expression? Leigh couldn't be sure. "Oh, they're not rejecting my application. He just suggested I wait until the next class, wait until after the baby."

Nick came around the chair, pulling her into his arms. "Oh, sweetheart, I know how disappointed you must be." He tucked her face into his shoulder, his fingers stroking through her hair. "But this is only a postponement."

Leigh stood, her arms rigid at her side, dreading what he might say next. He tilted her chin with his fingertips, his gaze tender, concerned.

"Why don't we take off early?"

As he spoke, his warm, moist breath stirred the tendrils of hair at her temple, and the wave of excitement it aroused added to her anger.

"I know just the thing to make you feel better," he murmured.

Her spine stiff with fury, she pushed out of his arms. "Is that the plan? Now that you've guaranteed I have to delay law school, you'll take me home and use sex to make me forget?"

"What the hell are you talking about?"

She glared at him. "If this isn't some kind of replay. So many times Brad used those same words, so many times he—" She shook her head. "Why do I bother? You don't understand any more than he did."

She turned and rushed into her office, Nick close behind her. He caught her by the arm and swung her around. "I'm not your damned ex-husband, Leigh." Nick gripped her shoulders, his fingers like steel on her arms. "I'm not offering sex as a bribe. And what do you mean, now that I've guaranteed you have to wait to start school?"

"Dr. Porter told me the reason they want me to withdraw my application is because my boss told him about my pregnancy."

"And, of course, you suspected me of some kind of double-dealing." He stood there, his body still, waiting, his expression smoldering.

She gave him a tight smile, bitterness sharp on her tongue. "Who else has spent months trying to convince me that I didn't need to be a lawyer to be fulfilled? Who has questioned every decision I make? Who offers his opinion, asked for or not, on everything? I can't debate whether to get white bread or whole wheat that you're not right there, putting in your two cents."

"We're not talking about something so minor as which bread you're going to buy, Leigh. What we're talking about is your obsessive fear that if you let yourself trust me, you will become a puppet, dancing to my command."

He pulled her closer, his thighs hard against hers. She pushed with her hands against his unyielding chest, uneasy with the sexual tension his anger aroused in her.

"But what it all comes down to, angel, is you have to decide." His voice was low, rumbling with a thread of danger twined through his words. "Can you trust me or not? I can't prove I didn't talk to Dr. Porter."

She closed her eyes against his hot, intense stare. "No, you can't, can you?"

"But *I* can."

Leigh pivoted toward the sound of the quiet voice and saw Drew standing in the partially open door to the main office. He edged into the room, closed the door and leaned against it, his expression grave.

"I didn't mean to eavesdrop," he said as he gestured toward the outer office. "But your argument got kind of loud."

Nick released Leigh's arms and stepped away from her. Drew walked to the desk and perched his hip on the corner. "Maggie told me about the call from Dr. Porter. I'm afraid I'm the one who let the cat out of the bag, Leigh. When he asked me for a personal recommendation, I was so eager to tell Dr. Porter what a great candidate you were, how much we were going to miss you while you were on maternity leave..."

Leigh flashed a glance at Nick, but his thoughts were shuttered from her by his half-closed lids. She felt a dull pain in the pit of her stomach. Oh, God, she had done it again.

"I never thought about the effect your pregnancy would have on your application," Drew continued. "I'm sorry, Leigh."

"Of course." Leigh knew her smile wobbled as much as her voice. "I never thought, but in a way, you're as much my boss as Nick, aren't you?"

She turned to Nick, her hand reaching out for him. "Nick . . . ?" The word hurt her throat.

He evaded her touch. "Let's leave it for now, Leigh." The corner of his mouth quirked and he slanted her a mocking look. "I think we've aired enough of our differences in public."

He headed for his office, motioning for Drew to join him. "Come on, partner, and I'll show you what we ended up with on the Morrison deal."

Drew, with a doubtful glance at Leigh, preceded Nick through the doorway.

"Nick, please . . ." She walked toward him, her hand raised in protest, but his cold stare halted her.

"Later, Leigh."

He closed the door, and she stared at the unyielding wooden barrier, her palms damp, as chills rippled down her spine. Silence lay like a black velvet cloak around her shoulders, heavy, dark.

Oh, my God, she thought. *Nick will never forgive me now.*

Nine

Leigh, with her chin propped on her palm, took a bite and grimaced. Somehow, a banana split made with low-fat yogurt and fresh fruit didn't comfort her like a real one would have. And, she decided, stirring the melting mess, a banana split without chocolate syrup was sheer blasphemy. She sighed and pushed away the bowl.

She sat at the kitchen table and stared into the newly finished dining room. For once she couldn't feel the pride she normally had for how well both rooms had turned out. In fact, since Nick's return this morning when she'd attacked him without cause, she wasn't sure she'd ever feel proud again. If only she'd been able to talk to Nick alone. If only she'd— Leigh sighed again and twirled the spoon in the yogurt. What was the use of debating *"what ifs"*? The simple fact was she'd allowed her fear of commitment to create a wedge between her and Nick.

"Leigh!"

She jerked her head as she heard Nick's shout emphasized by the slamming front door. Her heartbeat speeded up, and she wiped suddenly damp palms against her slacks. He'd come. Angry, but at least he was here, with her.

"I...I'm in here, Nick." She fought to control her voice. She had to stay calm. This might be her one chance to save her future. All their futures.

She stood, her back against the table, and watched as he moved toward her. He appeared like a dark flame against the radiant June sunlight pouring through the patio doors, brightening the muted earth colors in the dining room. In his charcoal gray suit with his tie loosened and the top button of his white shirt undone, he made her heart ache. Why did she feel a need to preserve each moment with him like a tiny time capsule?

"We are going to have this out, once and all." He laid his briefcase on the table with enough force to rattle her dish.

Leigh felt her eyes widen as she dropped back into her chair. "Nick, I—"

"No." He brought his hand down in a slashing movement. "I don't want to hear any more crap about your ex-husband. I am not Brad Townsend, and I'm tired of taking that bastard's punishment."

She opened her mouth to answer, and he stopped her with one piercing glare. "Right from the start, you've been like a porcupine, all rolled up with your spines extended, ready to defend yourself against all enemies."

He paused, silently daring her to deny his accusation. Mute, she laced her fingers together in her lap and waited. She sensed the safety valve on his anger had finally blown, and nothing on earth was going to stop him from speaking his mind.

"Leigh, I can understand how leaving a bad marriage left you doubting yourself. But, I promise, you're more woman than most men could imagine. You're strong and bright and spirited. You know how to set a goal and meet it."

Leigh felt a tight knot loosen inside her. He placed his palms on the table and leaned toward her, the planes of his face like granite, his breath sweet and warm against her face.

"You don't need me or anyone to validate you as a person." His voice dropped and caressed her senses like black velvet. "But you do need me to love you. You need me to experience life with you. To fight and make up with you. To share your worries and your triumphs. You need everything that is in me to give, just as I need everything that's in you to give."

Like an unlocked shackle, the last doubt dropped from her heart. Here was no selfish, manipulative man who got his identity by keeping a woman subordinate. Nick was like an oak tree, its roots deep in the soil, able to shelter a woman without denying her the sunshine to grow.

"You're right." She laughed softly as his expression turned wary. "I'm one hell of a woman and you—" she grasped his strong forearms, tilted her head and brushed her lips over his "—you're the man who made me see it."

Nick straightened and eyed her doubtfully. "It can't be that easy. I expected to have to fight with you. No speeches about how you don't need anyone? No harangues about meeting your goals before you commit to a relationship?"

She stood and slid her hand up his arm, stroking her fingers over his stubble-roughened jaw, his firm lower lip. "I've already made myself the woman I wanted to be. I just didn't recognize her until I saw her through your eyes, through your love."

He smiled against her fingers. "You certainly took long enough. So we're agreed? You're a woman worth loving?"

"Yes, and you are one sensitive man."

"Well, that's not exactly the word I'd use." He settled his weight on one leg, his hip cocked and a lazy, wicked grin on his face. "But I don't mind you thinking I'm sexy. Now, how about a real welcome home?"

She choked on her laughter and stepped into his waiting arms. His lips were fierce, demanding. Hot desire sealed her to him, her breasts crushed to his powerful chest. He cradled the curve of her abdomen into the arch of his body. His arms supported her weight while his hands, warm and solid, tangled in her hair. Leigh wanted to absorb him, all of him. His taste, his strength, his love. Never had she wanted him so much and never had she felt so poignantly what losing him would mean. She feared what would happen when she finally told him about the baby.

Nick felt her settle into his embrace, and fire seared through his groin. She opened her lips to his teasing tongue, and his body tightened as he felt the silken strands of her hair slip through his fingers. He cupped her head and stroked her satiny skin with his thumbs as her light floral scent floated around him. He felt the frantic pulse in her soft throat that seemed to echo the pounding in his ears. As he swept his hand over the sweet curves of her hips and thighs, he watched desire cloud her eyes. Her hands fluttered over his chest, and she ran her tongue over her dewy lips.

"Nick...Nick," she whispered, her voice husky. "Wait. I have to tell you something. We have to talk about—"

"We've done enough talking. Oh, honey, I've missed you. Eight days without you is eight days too long." He stroked his tongue along her tender skin. "We'll talk tomorrow."

"B...b...but—"

He swept her up in his arms, her body molding itself warmly against him. "Not now, Leigh. I don't want to think about anything but loving you tonight."

He carried her into her dim bedroom. The late-afternoon sun peeked through the closed miniblinds, twinkling off the brass fittings of the oak furniture. He set her on her feet and ripped back the turquoise comforter, scattering the colorful throw pillows on the floor. Then he turned to the pleasurable task of undressing her. The expression in her eyes intrigued him...desire, love, doubt. He frowned and stroked her velvety cheek. "Honey? What's wrong?"

She searched his face, and he had the feeling she was in pain. Then she closed her eyes, shook her head and rubbed her face against his hand. "Just love me, Nick."

He nestled her face in his palms and possessed her mouth. Her unfettered response sent lightning sizzling along his nerves, and he slid his fingers down to her top button.

"No, I want to undress you," she whispered. She brushed his hands aside and tugged at his loosened tie. "I'm going to pack eight nights of loving into one."

Her moist lips trailed a scalding path over every inch of skin she exposed. She teased his flat nipple with her tongue, and Nick gritted his teeth. He sensed her need to dominate. Never before had she been so eager, so voracious in her passion. Her hunger astounded him, and he groaned as he held himself fiercely in check, fought to let her have her way. Faint tremors rippled along his skin, and he gasped as she opened the zipper on his pants.

"Oh, God, *cara.* You're killing me."

"Not yet," she murmured as she slipped her fingers beneath the waistband of his briefs and captured his arousal. "But I will."

She caressed him, and he was fascinated by the stark beauty of her face, taut with ecstasy. Just when the tension in his body told him he was fast approaching the edge, she slid her hands around his thighs and slipped his clothes off his hips. She nibbled her way down his stomach, the rhythm of her busy tongue inciting his most primitive drive. She lightly massaged the tight muscles of his legs, and he felt his skin tingle under her palms.

Nick gripped her shoulders and when her heated breath sighed across his rigid length, he pulled her to her feet. "No," he grated, his voice harsh in his tight throat. "If you do that, I will never last." He fumbled for the buttons of her blouse, and the feel of her increased pulse at her throat filled him with elation. "Now it's my turn." Determined to make her ache as much as he did, he forced himself to slowly peel off each article of clothing, tasting, sipping at her supple flesh.

He hesitated long enough to pay full homage to her breasts, sucking her nipples until they stood rosy and glistening. He knelt and feasted on her navel. Every time his tongue ravaged the small indentation, she moaned and kneaded his shoulders.

"Ni...i...ck!"

Her wail was a plea, a command, and he answered both. He swept her onto the bed and entered her in one swift thrust. She quickly caught his rhythm, and he lost himself in the pulsing heat that surrounded him. Her body convulsed with tiny explosions and triggered his own release. All time and space contracted, then expanded with a white-hot glare. There were no boundaries, no limits . . . just the sense of uncharted frontiers.

Slowly Leigh became aware of the world around her—the feel of Nick's rugged weight covering her, the musky scent of his sleek skin. She kissed his jaw and tasted a salty dampness. He lifted himself on his elbows, and she felt him brush the tangled hair from her cheek with gentle fingers.

"Tears, cara?" he murmured as he nuzzled her earlobe.

"The good kind. The kind that come from more pleasure than a body can hold." Unwilling to part from him, she tightened her arms around his waist when he attempted to roll off her. "No, I want to hold you for a while longer."

"I'm too heavy for you." He turned them until he lay at her side, his head cradled against her breasts. He curled his arm around her waist, his breath warm against her skin. "There, now I'm home."

She watched the last of the sun mute the light in the room to dusk as she lay and listened to his breathing slow to a steady rhythm. A sense of peace surrounded them, and she wanted to go on forever, holding him, letting the busy world spin by outside this special sanctuary. But she had to tell him. She'd been a coward for too long.

"Nick?" she whispered, her voice hushed in her tense throat.

A soft snore answered her, and she peered into his sleeping face. She noted the faint bruising under his eyes and smiled. If she knew her Nick, he'd worked too many hours while he was in Oregon. Tears blurred the sight of his relaxed features, his dark hair tumbled around his broad forehead. She held him closer, rubbing her cheek against the coarse, yet soft strands.

Okay, maybe she was being selfish, she thought fiercely. Once she told him the truth, she knew it would destroy whatever life she might have made with him. And she would tell him . . . but tomorrow. Tonight she would keep for herself, to collect one last memory. Tonight she would clasp him in her arms, protect him from the pain she knew was coming.

Nick muttered in his sleep and snuggled closer. She brushed a kiss across his brow, then held him and watched the room grow dark as silent tears rolled down her face.

Leigh made one final cut, then pried the grapefruit apart and placed the halves on small, blue-flowered plates. She tilted her head and frowned at the fruit. One piece was definitely smaller than the other, she decided, and the fluted edges looked a little ragged.

"What the heck, Nick always eats more than I do, anyway," she muttered as she set the plates on the table. She inspected the settings, then nodded in satisfaction. Fifteen more minutes and the two-cheese casserole in the oven would be ready. English muffins were in a heated basket, and the coffee was hot and black. Not bad for a woman who couldn't cook three months ago. Now all she had to do was get Nick.

She'd been alone when she'd awakened that morning. Lying in the rumpled bed, memories of the incredible night before had had her almost purring in a lazy feeling of well-being. But the sound of Nick whistling in the nursery had reminded her of her vow. Now, here she stood, her heart thumping and her palms sweaty, afraid to leave her sunlit kitchen.

She glanced once more at the table and felt the knot in her stomach tighten. There was nothing left to delay her. She could only hope her mother was right, that it was easier to deal with a well-fed man. Taking a deep breath that failed to calm her, she walked to the nursery.

The soft, early-morning light poured through the un-curtained window. Leigh paused in the open doorway and watched Nick as he rubbed wax with a cloth into the shiny veneer of the refinished rocking chair. As he knelt on the floor, his worn jeans were tight against his muscular thighs. Leigh let her gaze wander over the play of muscles in his bare chest as he polished the rich wood.

"The man who sold you that chair certainly wouldn't recognize it." She leaned against the jamb, her arms crossed in front of her. Nick looked up, and the heady power of his smile pierced her. Need instantly swamped her, and she forced herself to push away thoughts of luring him back to bed. "No one would believe we got it at a flea market."

"Turned out pretty good, didn't it?" He stroked one final time along the front stretcher of the rocker, then leaned back and examined his work. "I can't wait to see you and the baby in it."

He stood, and sunlight danced through the dark whorl of hair above the waistband of the jeans slung low on his hips. Unable to help herself, Leigh felt her resolve slip as she walked toward him. She desperately sought for some way to bring her unruly thoughts under control. But somehow, all she could think of was how his muscular frame fitted against hers when they made love.

"God, you're beautiful," he muttered as he slipped his arms around her waist and nuzzled the sensitive area behind her ear. "Just the smell of you makes me hard. And the taste of your skin . . ."

She felt a weakness seep through her legs as she felt his rigid length against her stomach. Oh, Lord, if she wasn't careful, she'd let herself be distracted as she was last night. For a moment she resented he could be so carefree while she was tense, but realized that to Nick this was just any other morning. She leaned back and pushed against his shoulders. "None of that now. Brunch will be ready in a few minutes."

"Let's put it on hold."

"Not after all the work I went through. Get your mind on something else."

"Like what?" He gave her a wicked grin as he kneaded her hips with his strong hands. "Should we discuss how the Kansas City Royals are doing in the playoffs?"

"Well, for one thing..." She searched her tumbled thoughts for something that would take his attention off seduction. She watched her fingertip trace the long, thin scar hidden in the thick mat of fur on his chest. "Every time I've asked you about this, you've always given me a flip answer. Come on. How about the truth for a change."

"It's no big deal. I had open-heart surgery." He captured her hand and brought her fingers to his mouth.

"Open heart surgery?" The feel of his warm, moist breath sent tingles skittering down her spine, and she forced herself to ignore them. "When?"

"When I was a month old. I was born with a heart defect."

She felt encased in ice as fear swept over her, and she gripped his hand with numb fingers. "What?"

Nick cupped her face with his other hand and forced her stare from the scar to his face. "I'm okay, honey. I was sickly as a child, but there's nothing wrong with me now."

"But surgery on a tiny baby?"

"I was born with the large vessels of my heart transposed." Leigh gasped and he pulled her into his arms. "Actually, in a way, my surgery was a blessing. When my sister Angie's oldest was born, they had a pediatric cardiologist on standby. We wouldn't have even known to watch for the defect if it hadn't been for my problem."

His words added to her horror. She clutched him, her whole body shaking. "Y-y-you don't understand. My baby could—"

"No!" Nick's arms tightened around her. "I know what you're thinking, but it's not going to happen to Sweetpea. My heart defect has nothing to do—"

"It does!" She pushed away and raked her hands through her hair. "It's your baby, too!" She covered her mouth with both hands, her stomach lurching as if in a runaway elevator. Oh, sweet Lord, how could she just blurt out the truth?

Nick frowned and shook his head. "What did you say?" She stepped back and watched as suspicion evolved in his eyes. He grasped her wrists, uncovering her lips. *"What did you say?"*

"It's your baby." Her throat was harsh, parched. She flinched as his grip tightened. "You're the father," she whispered.

"That's not possible. You've been pregnant since December. We didn't make love until March."

"No...no." She heard the confusion in his voice and ran her tongue over her dry lips. She had to help him understand. She had to make him believe her. She locked her gaze with his. "We made love after the Christmas party."

His fingers tightened on her wrists, and she gasped. He looked down, then dropped her hands, turned and walked to the window. "I don't remember much of that party. Just pieces..." He rubbed his temple with his fingers as he stared out into the morning.

"We'd been dancing." She watched him, her heart pounding in slow heavy beats. "You kept calling me your Christmas angel."

"You were dressed in red." He looked at her, his brow furrowed in thought. "I keep having these...these images. A star...something about a star."

A small, breathless laugh escaped her. "You called my birthmark your Christmas star when you found it." She waited, her muscles tense, but his expression remained bewildered. "We sneaked away from the party. You told me you were claiming me as an early Christmas present and you wanted to unwrap me in private."

For a moment he stared at her, blank surprise clouding his eyes. Then his gaze dropped to her abdomen, and for the rest of her life, she'd never forget the expression of awe in his eyes. She knew what he was feeling. Hadn't she felt the same way when the baby had moved the first time? As if all the love in the universe was focused in the center of her body?

She released the breath she hadn't realized she'd been holding as his gaze returned to her face and she saw belief...and a gathering storm in his eyes. He frowned, his dark eyebrows forbidding over his narrowed eyes. His mouth suddenly grim, he advanced on her and she swallowed against the tension in her throat.

"And you were never going to tell me, were you, Leigh?"

"Nick—"

"All these months and you never once hinted I was the father." He grabbed her shoulders and pulled her toward him until she could see his dilated pupils. "Here I was, doing my damnedest to give you the space you asked for, and all the time you were making choices about my baby. Choices I should have been involved in."

"If you'd just let me explain—"

"And you were so determined to make your goals, you were going to give away my baby without saying a word to me, weren't you?"

"Yes . . . no . . . I mean—" She pushed against his chest. "If only you would give me a chance to explain—"

"I must be a glutton for punishment." A muscle twitched in his cheek. "I always involve myself with women who are ambitious. And that's what it all comes down to, isn't it, Leigh? You were so determined to meet your destiny, you were willing to shatter our future."

His hands tightened, but she barely felt the pain. His anger seemed to fill the room, pressing down on her like the suffocating stillness before a storm.

"But what I find the hardest to forgive is how you endangered the baby. If the doctor had known about my heart defect, he would have insisted on checking for it."

"But . . . but, I didn't know."

"You didn't know because you were too wrapped up in what you wanted. You didn't think of anyone else . . . not me and certainly not the baby."

She closed her eyes against his accusing stare. Oh, God, what he said was true. She'd never considered that telling Nick meant more than informing him of his paternity. It also meant giving the doctor a full medical history. If anything was wrong, it would be her fault.

Nick thrust her away. "I've got to get out of here. I can't breathe." He pushed past her and hurried out of the nursery.

"Nick . . . please, where are you going?"

He turned at the opened front door and studied her. She stood in the hallway, one hand pressed protectively against her stomach. She could feel the baby moving, almost as if he felt her agitation. For an instant she thought Nick would come to her, hold her, and ease the torment in her heart.

"Going?" His mouth twisted and she shivered at the bleak expression in his eyes. "I'm not going anywhere, Leigh. I'm already there . . . at the gateway to hell."

He stomped out the door, slamming it behind him.

Nick sat, his back against the tree, and pulled his feet up. He wrapped his arms around his knees and watched the fiery sun set on the far side of the lake, for once unmoved by the soothing quietness around him. He always came to this spot at Keystone Lake when he was troubled, but today he didn't think anything would calm the demons loosened in him.

In the hours since leaving Leigh, he'd been trying to remember the Christmas party, but all he could come up with was fragments. The red-tinged clouds floating over the water reminded him of the teddy he had stripped off Leigh the night of the Christmas party. For a moment he was back in the hotel room, dancing to the music of a late-night movie as he slowly undressed Leigh amid laughter and kisses. The feel of her satin skin under his lips. The way she combed her long, slender fingers through the hair on his chest. He groaned and leaned his head against his knees. If it hadn't been for that spiked punch reacting with his medication, he would remember more than just traces of that night. But the real deception had been Leigh's.

He'd been patient with Leigh . . . tried to be supportive. He'd bent over backward to keep from interfering in her life, even when he didn't agree with her decisions. And how did she reward him? By lying to him. And that's what it came down to, lying by omission.

Anger was acrid in his mouth, and he stood, striding down the slope to the water's edge. He stepped carefully over the rocks, ignoring the rhythmic waves that washed over his bare feet.

All these months he'd lost one of the joys of fatherhood. Because Leigh had kept quiet, he'd been cheated out of sharing a pregnancy with the woman he loved. Oh, she'd reluctantly let him help as a friend, but knowing he was the father put a whole different slant on things. There were expectations he'd always had whenever he'd thought of being a father, and Leigh had denied him all of them. Well, no more. From now on he was taking a larger role in his baby's life, and if Leigh didn't like it, too damn bad.

A solitary hawk winged overhead, and Nick watched until it was out of sight. How much Leigh was like the bird—alone, independent, fierce in her pride. But even the hawk worked with a mate when there were young involved. Leigh hadn't learned this detail yet, Nick thought. But she would, and the time was now. His mind made up, he headed for his abandoned shoes.

Leigh's eyes were dry and burning as she watched the glow from the security light in her backyard flicker through the branches of a maple tree. A chill raced up her back, and she clutched the quilt tighter around her as she huddled deeper into the rocking chair. The darkened nursery matched her desolate thoughts, and she wished she could ease the heavy lump in her throat. But she hadn't been able to cry, not in all the hours since Nick had stormed out of the house.

Why had she waited so long to tell Nick? Why hadn't she told him as soon as she realized she loved him? She leaned her head against the back of the chair, closed her eyes and sighed. She'd never looked at it from Nick's point of view, and now, all too clearly, she understood what she'd lost.

The hall light flashed on and she stiffened, turning her head toward the door. Nick stood silhouetted in the glare, his expression hidden from her. She swung her feet to the floor and watched as he crossed the room and leaned against the crib. He was dressed in black jeans and T-shirt, his hands thrust in the pockets of a leather jacket. He looked rugged, unyielding, and Leigh felt a primitive thrill as she viewed his air of restrained power.

"Tell me one thing." His voice was cold and harsh. "Once I knew you were pregnant, why didn't you tell me the baby was mine?"

Leigh swallowed. She didn't recognize this Nick. She'd seen him angry before, but his temper had always been hot, like his Italian nature. It flashed with the intensity of lightning and then was gone. She'd never seen him like this, frigid, controlled, his eyes chilling her with an opaque blankness.

"I asked a simple enough question, Leigh. Why didn't you tell me the baby was mine?"

"B...b...because I was—" She ran her tongue over her dry lips. "I was afraid you would bulldoze me into marriage, take over my life."

"So you decided to keep quiet and give away my baby."

Somehow he made her sound calculating and uncaring. "At first, but I changed my mind. I decided—"

"Oh, once again *you* decided."

"Nick, try to understand. When I first found out about the baby, I panicked. You don't know what it was like when my marriage ended. Brad had spent money without any thought of tomorrow. Everything we'd bought was repossessed. Creditors hounded me daily for payment. I was twenty years old, destitute, and humiliated at what a fool I'd been."

"What does that have to do with now?" Nick gestured to the freshly remodeled room. "You've put your life back together. You're not a poor, scared little girl anymore."

She eased her grip on the arms of the rocker and tried to relax. "I was when I found out about the baby." She spoke carefully, desperate to make him understand. "All I could think of was if something went wrong, if my life fell apart again, I wouldn't be the only one in trouble. This time I would also have a dependent child."

"You had me. You knew I loved you. You knew I wanted you and the baby, even though I thought he was another man's. I would have married you the minute I knew the baby was mine.''

She winced at his use of the past tense. ''Oh, yes, I knew you'd do the 'right thing.' But don't you see? I didn't *know* you loved me. In fact, I'm not even sure I believed in love then.''

Nick walked to the window and stared into the dark. ''So you just decided to give the baby up for adoption and go on with your life.''

''At the time I thought adoption would be best for the baby. What did I know about being a mother? How could I take care of an infant while I worked and went to school?''

The faint light from the outside threw his profile in sharp relief, and Leigh saw him quirk the corner of his mouth. He turned, braced his hands on the windowsill and leaned back, crossing his ankles. ''Well, I'll make it easy for you, Leigh. The first thing we're going to do is get another sonogram and make sure the baby is okay.''

''I've already done that. I called my doctor after you left.''

He hesitated, his mouth softening momentarily. Then he nodded.

''Okay. Next, you quit your job, so you won't have to be concerned about working.''

''What?'' She rose so quickly the rocking chair scooted across the floor.

''Oh, don't worry about how you're going to support yourself. My child is going to carry my name. We'll be married as soon as I can make the arrangements. As my wife, you'll stay home and I'll maintain my family like any loving husband should.''

Her temper soared at his sarcastic words. She swung away from him and stalked a few paces. ''I knew this would happen. I knew if I told you about my pregnancy you would try to take over my life.'' She faced him, her fists on her hips. ''Well, I won't have it, Nick. I won't let you come in here and issue orders.''

His hands clenched, he advanced until he towered over her. Leigh tensed, ready for an argument.

"You have no choice. As far as I'm concerned, you lost all rights to my consideration when you failed to tell me the truth. You will do what I tell you, like it or not."

"Like hell I will. I'm not quitting my job."

"You'd rather be the butt of office gossip? Everyone watching us and wondering?"

She winced, and her temper abated slightly. Nick was right. She couldn't see herself facing the speculation that would sweep through the office with the speed of a wild-fire. But she resented giving in to his demands.

"I won't quit, but I will go on maternity leave," she conceded grudgingly.

"And after the baby's born?"

"I'll face that when the time comes."

He frowned, but she glared at him, daring him to argue.

"As you wish," he said as he shrugged. "I really don't care. Once the baby is born, we'll get a divorce. Then the only thing you'll have to share with me is a child. You can get on with your own life. You can build a career. You can go to hell for all I care."

She gasped at the cruelty of his words, and her brief moment of mutiny died. How had they ever gotten to the point where they'd wanted to hurt each other? What had happened to the gentle Nick she'd known? He turned toward the door and she laid her hand on his arm, forcing him to stop.

"Nick, wait. We can't do this to each other."

He glanced at her hand, then returned his gaze to her face. "What did you have in mind, Leigh?"

She forced herself to slow her ragged breathing. She sensed she had only one chance to reach him. If she could just keep her temper, if she could get him to talk calmly, maybe they could resolve this without any further pain.

"Why don't I make some coffee?" She tightened her grip on his arm. "We could sit down and talk, work things out."

He stared at her thoughtfully, and she felt the knot in her throat ease.

"What kind of things?" His tone was bland, and a current of uneasiness trickled down her spine.

"Things? Well, you know . . ." She faltered, not understanding the peculiar gleam in his eyes. "I mean, after all we've shared . . ."

"Yes? After all we've shared . . . ?" His voice was a low, velvet purr.

She wet her parched lips and forced a smile. "I mean, you say you love me. I can't believe all those feelings are gone and . . ." Leigh cursed herself for being a coward. Nick deserved to hear her say it. He'd been patient long enough. "And I love you, Nick."

She waited, her blood pounding in her throat as Nick's gaze searched her eyes.

"I've waited a long time to hear you say you love me, Leigh." He gently removed her hand from his arm and stepped away. "But after what you've done, the way you kept the truth from me, I'm afraid I don't believe you."

A cold agony gripped her heart, and Leigh clasped her arms around her waist against the pain. He didn't believe her. And now she'd lost him.

He headed for the door and she took a step after him. "Nick!"

He paused, looking over his shoulder. "Are we getting married or not?"

Wasn't that what she wanted . . . to marry him, build a life with him? Didn't she want him as a husband, as the father of her baby, as a lover? Okay, so this wasn't the way she'd hoped they'd marry . . . the way she'd dreamed. If she accepted, at least she would have time to show him that she *did* love him.

"Yes," she whispered, wishing he'd give her one sign she wasn't depending on a false hope.

He nodded. "Then there's nothing left to say." Like a wisp of smoke he was gone.

And Leigh stood alone in the empty nursery, listening to the beat of her empty heart.

Ten

―――――

"'**B**out time you got back." Drew grinned as he stood in the doorway of the library, a thick law book in his hand. "I know we're lenient about running overtime on lunches around here, but isn't three hours a bit long?"

As usual, bedlam reigned in the office. Phones rang while the fax slid out reams of information. Over the soft click of computer keys, Leigh could hear the lighthearted razzing of her co-workers and felt her face flush. Oh, Lord, wait until they find out why we're late, she thought. She glanced over her shoulder and saw Nick approaching. He was followed by Maggie, a coffee cup in her hand.

"Could I have your attention, please?" The noise level dropped slightly at Nick's request.

Maggie's eyes widened as she raised an eyebrow, but Leigh ignored the questions in her friend's eyes and focused on Nick. He stood next to Leigh, his hands in his pockets, his expression stern and unyielding. Dread clenched Leigh's stomach, and she swallowed the hard lump in her throat. She'd never live through this fiasco.

"What's going on, Nick?" Drew looked at her, then Nick. "You look grim. What's the trouble?"

"Leigh and I were married an hour ago, and starting the end of the week, she'll be taking her maternity leave."

A babble of voices broke out at Nick's terse statement, and Leigh found herself wrapped in a bearhug and bussed firmly by Drew.

"Best of luck, Leigh." Drew's voice boomed in her ear. He released her and grabbed Nick's hand. "Congratulations, you ol' reprobate. 'Bout time you came to your senses. Anyone could see you belonged together."

"Thank you." Nick smiled, but no one would have taken him for a happy groom. "Leigh and I appreciate your good wishes, but we would prefer to keep the celebrating at a minimum."

"But...but—"

Leigh winced at Drew's obvious bewilderment but recognized Nick's bulldozer methods. He wanted to get this over with, and no one was going to stand in his way.

"Connie," Nick said as he turned to the young blonde. "Would you finish what you're doing, then work full-time with Leigh? That way you can start your new job next week."

Connie gaped at him a moment, then nodded.

"Good. I guess we'd better get back to work."

Leigh watched him walk into his office and close the door, leaving her behind to face the silence. How dare he? He acted as if she'd forced him into this marriage. She eyed her co-workers and felt her spirits droop. Damn, now what was she supposed to do? She could see the speculation, the questions she didn't know how to answer.

Taking the coward's way out, she smiled weakly. "Excuse me, but I need to freshen up." She hurried into the restroom and sagged against the vanity. Her tense features reflected back from the mirror and she closed her eyes.

"Married," she whispered, rolling the word around in her mouth, tasting it. Even now she could hardly believe it. She wished she knew what she felt...excitement...

confusion . . . what? A harsh chuckle forced its way out of
her throat. Definitely not joy.

"What the hell's going on, Leigh?"

She opened her eyes and saw Maggie's worried reflection next to hers in the mirror.

"You heard Nick." Leigh bent and splashed cold water
on her face, then dried it with a paper towel. "We got
married."

"I heard him. Now tell me the details. I assume you told
him about the baby."

Leigh pulled her comb from her purse and tugged it
through her hair, silently cursing her shaking hand. "Yes,
I told him."

"And . . . ?"

Leigh hesitated. "I've never seen Nick so angry."

"But you got married."

Leigh dropped the comb back into her handbag, turned
to face the older woman and quirked her mouth. "No, we
agreed to a business merger. The dry, emotionless ritual we
went through could hardly be called a wedding."

Maggie grimaced. "That bad, huh?"

"Worse. The courthouse air conditioner was broken
down, so the heat was murder. I felt like I'd been melted
and remolded. The judge hurried through the ceremony
because he only had a few minutes between cases. Our wit-
nesses were two bored clerks who obviously wanted everything over with so they could go to lunch."

"Surely you're exaggerating."

"You think so? I stood there, sticky, wilted with my hair
standing on end and Nick beside me like a stone statue. He
didn't even touch me except to slide the ring on." She closed
her eyes and shuddered. "I felt like the bride of Franken-
stein."

"Oh, honey." Maggie grasped Leigh's hands. "You've
gotten off to a rocky start, but you'll see. It'll all work out."

"I wish I believed that," Leigh whispered, clinging to
Maggie. She tilted her head back and blinked away the tears
that threatened to fall. "When I agreed to this marriage, I
thought Nick would get over his anger, at least long enough

for me to convince him I love him. But, Maggie, after we had the blood tests, he went to Dallas for that business meeting, and when he came back, I never saw him except at the office and then only briefly.''

''Did you go to his apartment?''

''Yes, but he was never home. He never replied to my messages on his answering machine. Then like a whirlwind, with only a ten-minute warning from him, I find myself in front of the judge, participating in the wedding from hell.''

''Then you aren't living together yet?''

''No.'' Leigh dropped Maggie's hands, folded her arms around her waist and propped herself on the vanity. ''He's moving into the house tonight.''

''And the two of you will be alone.''

''So?''

''From what you're saying, tonight will be the first time you've spent any time together for a while. While you help him get squared away, you'll have plenty of time to talk.''

Leigh glanced at Maggie and Maggie arched an eyebrow.

''Just remember, Leigh. Nick may have orchestrated the wedding his way, but tonight it will be just the two of you. And it *is* your wedding night.''

''I doubt if that will make a difference.'' But it was something to think about, Leigh pondered as she left the ladies' room. By now, Nick's anger seemed to have gone from boiling to a simmer. Maybe if they had a quiet, unstressed evening together, they could solve all their problems. Plans seethed in her head as she and Connie settled in to work.

Despite how busy Leigh found herself, the afternoon seemed to creep by. Even the impromptu reception Maggie and Drew threw together at the end of office hours only increased her impatience to have the day over. Nick appeared to take the good-natured ribbing of their coworkers, but Leigh could tell from the expression in his eyes that he was simply going through the motions. At least she was grateful that no one except Maggie, and possibly Drew, knew the truth about their marriage.

As soon as she could, Leigh flew out of the office and hurried home. She threw one of Nick's veggie lasagnas into the oven, then took a quick shower. She would have liked to stay under the warm water spray, letting it relax her tense muscles, but she wasn't sure when Nick would arrive with his possessions.

An hour later she was ready. She examined the table, set with her best china and silver. The candles glowed softly over the last of the roses from her garden, and the aroma of lasagna gave a homey feel to the room. A sense of déjà vu swept over her as she looked at the ring she'd bought Nick before putting it beside his place setting. Here she was, planning to propose to him again. She hoped this time would go better than last.

The doorbell rang, and her heart stuttered in her chest. She caught a glimpse of her reflection in the mirror over the buffet and swept a trembling hand down her white silk top. She wished she could be wearing a peignoir, then laughed at herself. But being seven months pregnant and wearing sexy nightwear didn't go together. Besides, she wanted tonight to be an evening for repairing a torn relationship, not seduction. The doorbell rang again, and taking a deep breath, she went to let Nick in.

A pile of boxes was stacked on the porch and Nick was headed from his black sports car, two suitcases in his hands. She'd never seen him so casual, yet so virile. A twisted handkerchief acted as a headband, keeping his sweat-soaked hair off his brow. His muscular arms were bare under an old sweatshirt with the sleeves torn off, and his powerful body moved with grace. His faded cut-offs exposed strong thighs, lightly sprinkled with dark hair. After four days alone, her body tingled at the thought of him holding her tightly in his arms.

"Can I give you a hand?" She reached for the smaller suitcase he was carrying, but he turned aside.

"Thanks, but these are too heavy for you. If you'd just hold the storm door open, I can get everything."

His impersonal courtesy stood like a wall between them.

She opened the door wider and stood holding it as he brushed by her. His damp skin, smelling of hot summer nights, tantalized her, and her senses tingled with awareness—the sound of crickets in the yard, Junebugs darting into the porch light, the scent of fresh-cut grass. As she watched him walk down the hall, she took a moment to appreciate the way the soft denim molded his backside. The sight of him entering the spare bedroom jarred her out of her sensual haze, and she hurried after him.

"What are you doing?"

"Moving in."

"Here?"

She glanced around the sparsely furnished room. There was a faint mildew smell, left over from when the roof used to leak. An ancient twin bed and a bureau awaiting refinishing lined the walls, which were partially stripped of wallpaper. She had pulled up the old torn carpet, leaving behind remnants of the padding on a scarred wooden floor.

"You can't stay here," she said with a shudder. "You won't be comfortable."

He shrugged as he set the suitcases on the unmade bed. "It'll do until after the baby comes. You can't be alone, and since I'll have to move to a place that allows children, I might as well move in temporarily."

She followed him as far as the living room when he returned to the front porch, frustration churning her stomach.

"Nick, could you sit down and talk to me for a minute?" The oven timer sounded, and she gestured toward the kitchen. "At least take time to have dinner. We both missed lunch."

Nick walked to the dining room door and stared at the festive table. "A celebration dinner, Leigh?"

She clenched her teeth against his sarcastic tone. "I thought since we were married now, we should make the best of the situation. We can't live in a cold war."

He slumped against the jamb, and for the first time Leigh noticed the tired lines in his face. It was evident he hadn't slept any better in the past few days than she had.

"What did you have in mind? A cozy dinner, a quick romp in bed, and everything would be okay?" He crossed his arms against his broad chest and shook his head. "It doesn't work like that, Leigh. For the sake of the baby, I'll be here to help you through the rest of your pregnancy, but don't start thinking of this as a real marriage. It's clear we don't want the same things. Once I believed we could work out a compromise, but now I accept that the only thing we'll share is the baby."

"We share so much more."

"Like what? Honesty? Commitment?" He pushed away from the portal with his shoulders and shoved his hands in his pockets. "What I see is a woman who didn't tell me for seven months that she was pregnant with my child. I see a woman who is so determined to be independent she doesn't need me. Every day I'll wonder what important thing you're not sharing with me. Every time you advance in your career, I'll wonder whether you'll abandon me and the baby. I'll never be sure of you."

"Nick, I understand you might not trust me right now." A little daunted by his implacability, Leigh forced down the panic that threatened to choke her. "I admit I was wrong not telling you sooner. But I intend to show you that I *do* love you. I want you and Sweetpea, and I'll prove to you our marriage can work."

"Be my guest." He pulled his hands from his pockets and spread them, palms up. "But frankly, I don't think you're capable of the kind of commitment I want. Now, if you'll excuse me, I'd like to get the rest of those boxes in. I want to get everything moved tonight."

He headed for the front porch. She stood for a moment, sure there was something she could say, something she could do to break through his defensive shield. Doubt niggled at the back of her mind. What if it was over? What if they spent the next few months, living as roommates, and she couldn't convince him of how much she loved him?

She pushed her misgivings aside and served herself dinner. Always aware of the sound of him moving in and out of the house, she sat at the table, forcing herself to eat food that tasted like cardboard. Finally she sensed Nick behind her, but refused to face him, afraid he might see the tears threatening to fall.

"I'm leaving now." He hesitated and she held her breath, hoping he would relent and ask her to help him.

"Don't wait up for me. My brother-in-law is bringing his pickup to help me put my furniture in storage, and I'll probably be late."

She heard the door close behind him and abandoned any attempt to eat. The gala table mocked her as she watched the candles melt away. A lone petal dropped from the wilting roses. Never before had it bothered her to be alone, but now her solitary state sat on her shoulders like a millstone. She braced her elbows on the table and buried her face in her hands. The silence closed around her, weighing her down. What if she had to live without Nick forever?

"Tired?"

Leigh turned her gaze from the storm outside the car and examined Nick's rugged profile. She noted his tone was no more than courteous, but anything was better than the inflexibility he'd shown a month ago at the wedding. Remembering a time when he would have given her a tender smile, she felt tears prick her eyes.

"No, I'm not tired, but I need to make a stop, anyway, if you don't mind."

"Too much lemonade. Since you're eight months along, the baby doesn't leave you much room inside, does he? There's a truck stop a few miles down the road. Can you wait that long?"

"Yes, of course." She glanced at the wind-driven rain pounding onto the expressway. "I wonder if we should go to Lamaze tonight with this storm." She scanned the yellow-green clouds and frowned. "I don't like the look of that sky."

"Don't worry, Leigh. I'll get us there. I want to see that childbirth film."

As usual when they were alone, their conversation lapsed. The separation between her and Nick seemed wider than ever. Oh, Nick was the perfect husband. Always conscious of her health, he insisted on doing more than his share of the housework. But most evenings she spent alone watching television while Nick worked in his bedroom. She didn't even have the solace of working on the house, since Nick had forbidden any more remodeling for fear of what the hard work and chemical fumes might do to the baby.

At first Leigh had hoped time and proximity would soften Nick's anger. But night after night she lay in her lonely bed, aching, tormented by the knowledge of Nick only a few feet down the hall. It amazed her how much she missed him. Not just his lovemaking, but the little things about him that made him uniquely Nick. The sound of his laughter, the tender gleam in his eyes as he felt the baby move inside her, even his nagging her to drink just one more glass of milk.

She closed her eyes, leaned her head against the headrest and sighed, desolation heavy in her heart. The only bright spot in the past month, she concluded, was that the sonogram had proved there was nothing wrong with the baby.

A black pickup truck, horn blaring, whipped around the car and Leigh gasped.

"What the hell is that fool doing?" Nick snarled as he jerked the wheel to the right.

Leigh looked over her shoulder, then blinked and looked again. "It can't be..."

She stared straight into the jaws of hell. A tornado snaked along, oily black, with a cloud of debris at its base. She tried to speak, but her words were stuck in her throat. She watched as the funnel bore down on them, menacing, unrelenting.

"Nick!" She gripped his arm, her voice thin and shrill in her ears. "A tornado! It's on the ground."

He glanced in the rearview mirror and swore as he swerved to the side of the road and slammed on the brakes.

Leigh jerked against her seatbelt. "What are you doing?" She tightened her hold on him, her heart thumping so hard she thought she would choke. "There's the truck stop. We can make it if—"

"Are you crazy?" Beads of perspiration glistened on his brow, and a muscle twitched in his jaw. "We can't outrun a tornado." He slid along the seat and unclasped her seat belt before opening her door. "Now, damn it, get out."

Nudged by the pressure of his body, Leigh stumbled into the driving rain. Grass and leaves swirled around her, battering her from all directions. A crumpled beer can slammed into her abdomen, and she bent over, huddled against the car. She had to protect the baby. The wind seemed to suck her breath, even her thoughts from her.

"Come on, Leigh. We've got to move!" Nick shouted in her ear as he slipped his arm around her waist and pushed her away from the car.

Leigh floundered through the tangled weeds, her mind frozen with fear. A sharp pain slashed through her side and Leigh pressed her hand against it. Oh, God, was she going into labor? She gasped as her lungs burned with a lack of air. An empty fast-food sack flashed by her head and she flinched, then realized she was alone. Where was Nick? She screamed his name, but the word was torn from her lips.

She turned back, and a few feet behind her, she saw Nick on the ground, a large tree branch across his back. She stumbled to his side, dropped to her knees, and started pulling at the bough.

"'M okay." His expression dazed, he brushed at her hands. "Keep going."

"Not without you," she said, sobbing.

She pushed at the branch, then grabbed her belly with one hand as she felt a hot, tearing ache along the bottom. The muscles in her arm trembled as she pressed against the wood. Finally, with his help, she pushed the limb aside and he staggered to his feet, shaking his head. Blood trickled down the side of his face, and she lifted her hand toward his forehead.

"I'm okay." He grabbed her around the waist and loped down the incline. "Let's get the hell out of here."

He guided her into a large drainage ditch, then pushed her to her knees, crowding behind her as she crawled into the concrete culvert. The scent of rotted vegetable triggered nausea in a stomach already roiling. Running water soaked her skirt, but at least they were partially sheltered from the storm. She sat in the slimy mud at the bottom of the drain and leaned against the wall.

The roar of the approaching tornado drowned out the sound of her heartbeat, and Leigh gripped Nick's shirt. She buried her face against the hard, warm shelter of his chest and felt his strong arms circle her. He pressed her against the wall, covering her body with his, shielding her and the baby. His scent filled her head, and his weight crushed her. She closed her eyes, slid her arms around his waist and burrowed closer. She wanted to scream, but her throat was frozen. Maybe if she held on tightly enough, just maybe she could keep both Nick and the baby safe.

Reality fragmented into impressions. The cold, hard surface behind her...the suction of the wind pulling at her clothing, her hair...the shriek of tortured metal. And through it all, Nick...strong, unyielding. She felt a rumble in his chest and realized he was talking to her. She couldn't understand what he was saying, but she clung to the security he offered. In his arms, she could almost control the fear clawing at her throat.

After an eternity, Leigh realized she was hearing his words and raised her head, her gaze locked on his blood-streaked face. Her hands trembled as she ran them over his shoulders, down his arms, searching for injuries in the dim light. Her throat ached as if she'd been screaming, but she didn't remember making a sound.

"It's okay, Leigh. It's over." He cupped her face, warming her chilled skin as his gaze swept over her. "Are you all right?"

"Yes." She stared into his eyes, the concern in his voice starting a thaw along the edges of a heart that had been frozen in her chest for a month. She brushed away a twig caught in his tousled hair. "Oh, Nick, your head—"

"It's okay. The branch just clipped me." He pulled his handkerchief out of his pocket and dabbed at a cut in his hairline. "Why did you come back? You risked the baby's life."

Of course, she thought as her burgeoning hope died. She might have known his only care was for the safety of the baby.

"Everything's fine," she lied, ignoring the ache in her back and the mild cramp in her lower belly. "Let's get out of here."

She turned, and he grasped her arm, a frown on his face. "Leigh, wait a minute. I only meant—"

"I know what you meant," she said through gritted teeth. "As long as the baby's all right, nothing else matters, right? Well, as far as I'm concerned, you're *both* vital to me. Now, can we leave? I'd really like to go home."

"Leigh—"

She pushed herself away from the shelter of his arms and crawled out of the conduit. Rain pounded on her and Leigh shivered. She pulled at the muddy skirt, plastered to her backside, cold water dripping down her legs. Nick followed her, a scowl furrowing his brow.

"I've got to get you where it's warm and dry." He grasped her hand and guided her up the steep incline to the side of the road.

"Best idea I've heard today," she muttered, panting as she struggled in his wake.

When they reached the highway, she gaped at the chaos. Automobiles and trucks lay on their sides, tossed by the tornado like children's abandoned toys. In the far distance, she could hear the faint sound of a woman screaming. Trees lay splintered on the ground while metal power poles stood like eery twisted sculptures. Nick's car had disappeared.

"Damn." Nick clenched his jaw, then slipped off his suit jacket and tucked it around her shoulders. "Wait here. I see a patrol car down the highway."

He strode away, his rain-soaked shirt molded against his back. She sank down on a short cement post that formed part of the edgeway and wrapped her arms around her swollen abdomen. Nick's distinctive scent permeated his jacket, and she huddled into the lingering warmth.

She watched as traffic picked its way through the debris on the road. The rain eased to a drizzle, and the sun peeked through rapidly breaking clouds. She could see the backside of the storm, lightning flickering like snakes' tongues from the angry clouds while thunder growled in the distance. The odor of gasoline drifted on the newly washed breeze. Around her she heard men shouting amidst crying children. She knew she should go help, but her mind seemed numb. Her head ached and her stomach churned. She shuddered as she closed her eyes, drew in a breath and swallowed against the nausea.

"Leigh?"

She looked up. Through tear-blurred eyes, she saw Nick approaching with a highway patrolman. Nick kneeled, brushed away the hair entangled in her eyelashes, then tenderly kissed her temple.

"This officer's going to drive us to the hospital."

Leigh tried to smile at the policeman, but doubled over and moaned as a sharp pain pierced her. She fought against the black clouds edging her vision.

"Nick . . . oh, Nick . . . something's wrong."

She fell forward, but in an instant, she was caught up in Nick's arms. He held her tightly, his heart pounding under her ear as he carried her with ground-eating strides to a waiting patrol car.

"Oh, God, sweetheart, hold on. We'll get you to the hospital as quickly as we can."

Was he really as worried about her as his tense voice hinted? And had he really called her sweetheart? She wanted to ask him, but the shadow creeping over her showed no mercy. Another severe pain stabbed her and she gave in to the dark.

Eleven

Nick stood beside the gurney and held Leigh's limp hand. He wanted to take her in his arms, but was afraid he would awaken her. He settled for brushing her matted hair away from her pale face with his free hand. She had regained consciousness on the ride into the emergency room, but had been racked with labor pains. On their arrival, the staff had given Leigh some medicine that stopped the contractions, and she'd drifted into a light doze.

"Mr. Romano?"

Nick looked up and saw a short, rotund man in a wrinkled lab jacket with a stethoscope around his neck standing in the doorway of the examining room.

"I'm Dr. Michaels. Mrs. Romano's obstetrician is out of town and I'm covering for him." The doctor extended his hand and Nick took it, comforted by the alert expression in the other man's eyes despite his obvious fatigue. "How's she doing?"

Nick gave him a shaky smile. "You tell me, Doctor. That stuff they gave her seems to have stopped the labor, but other than that, I can't get any more information."

Dr. Michaels scanned the chart he held under his arm. "That's because we don't have all the answers yet. But here's what we've got so far. The Breathine injection seems to be holding the labor for now, but based on my experience, if a baby really wants to come, he will."

"But it's too soon for the baby. He's not due for another five weeks."

"We've done an amniocentesis, but the lab is swamped right now with all the tornado victims. If that shows the baby's lungs are ready, we will probably let the labor continue. The fetal heart tones are a little elevated, but he's not distressed, so we've got time to wait."

He hesitated, and Nick saw a shadow of doubt cross his face. "What else?"

"The intern reported some vaginal bleeding that concerns me."

A chilling fear numbed Nick's mind and sweat broke out in his palms. "What does that mean?"

"There are several possibilities. It's conceivable the placenta has torn loose slightly. If that's true, then we'll let the labor continue and be prepared for a premature birth."

"And if it's not the placenta?"

"It could be a simple vaginal bleed or... or there could be a uterine laceration. If that's the case, there's a risk of severe hemorrhage. We'd have to perform a C-section."

"Is Leigh in danger?" Nick could hardly force the words past his dry lips.

"I won't lie to you, Mr. Romano." Michaels reached up and squeezed Nick's shoulder. "It will be touch and go for a while."

A nurse stepped into the exam room and murmured a few words to the doctor, then activated the blood pressure machine already attached to Leigh's arm. Leigh stirred, and Nick held his breath, but she didn't awaken.

"We'll be moving your wife to the OB floor in a few minutes," Dr. Michaels reported.

Nick forced his gaze from Leigh's pale face and focused on the doctor. The other man smiled gently.

"I know you're worried, but she's fairly stable right now. Why don't you go with her, and while the nurses settle her in, they can tell you where to clean up and get into scrubs."

Nick nodded, then returned his gaze to Leigh. He barely noticed when the other two people left the room. All he could think about was that he might lose Leigh. How could he have imagined he could divorce her, live without her? Even at her most aggravating, she excited him. But he had let his anger, his hurt separate them.

"We're ready to move her upstairs, Mr. Romano."

Nick stepped away as an orderly moved Leigh's IV bag from the overhead hook to his shoulder and unlocked the wheels. Nick had to release Leigh's hand so the gurney would clear the door. As he followed the orderly through the crowded, noisy hall, he noticed a sheet-covered body in another exam room and stopped in horror. That could have been Leigh. If she died, his pride would be cold comfort. If only he had time to tell her, to show her how much he loved her. If only—

A gentle roll of thunder roused Leigh from sleep. She opened her eyes and saw a lazy rain trickle down the window, fracturing the gleam from highway lights into miniature rainbows on the glass. For a moment she forgot where she was. Then she caught sight of a pulsating red light and remembered. The oak veneer nightstand next to the bed was really a fetal heart monitor, and she was in a birthing room at Tulsa Regional Medical Center.

She turned onto her back, then closed her eyes and held her breath as a mild cramp gripped her abdomen. She fought her fear as she used the relaxation breathing she'd learned in Lamaze. Now that her labor was halted, she was determined not to let it start again. She sighed in relief, as the pain eased, and cuddled deeper into the covers. She heard a soft snore and opened her eyes.

Nick lay sleeping in a smoky blue recliner next to her bed, his dark hair tousled over his wide forehead. Leigh's heart twisted at the sight of him. Her gaze drifted over the long, inky lashes, his sensual mouth, now relaxed in sleep, and his squared jaw stubbled with an early morning beard. She smiled at the rumpled green scrubs he wore, but appreciated the way the V-neck top hinted at the thick pelt of hair on his chest. Her gaze moved back to his face, and she saw his eyes were open, watching her.

He leaned forward, forcing the recliner into an upright position, and picked up her hand, his thumb stroking the back of it.

"How are you feeling?" His voice was smoky with sleep, his smile tender.

Tears wet her lashes. He sounded like the old Nick, the one she'd fallen in love with before he learned about the baby. "Okay, so far. I think the medicine is working."

He glanced at the red digital numbers on the monitor and grinned. "Sweetpea says he's doing fine, too. His heartbeat is one hundred and thirty-two, well within the range the nurse said he should be. With luck, we're out of here by noon." He hesitated, his brow furrowed in thought. "Leigh, when we get home, we need to make some changes."

A shiver of apprehension rippled down Leigh's spine, and she pushed herself up in the bed, ignoring the soreness in her muscles. Another cramp, slightly stronger, clenched her middle, and she took a deep breath as her heart slammed against her rib cage in painful thuds. "Do you—" She couldn't get the words through her tight throat. She licked her dry lips and tried again. "You mean, you want the divorce immediately?" She was surprised how calm her voice sounded when, inside, her heart shattered.

Nick surged to his feet and moved next to the bed. "Divorce? No way, lady." He sat on the edge, clasped both her hands tightly and focused a dark, brooding gaze on her. "Leigh, I love you. And you say you love me. What I'm suggesting is that we make our marriage real."

"Oh, Nick," Leigh whispered, her pulse beating with a wild cadence in her throat. Joy rippled through her and blocked coherent thought.

"I've been wrong," he continued. "I was so angry at you for not telling me about the baby I did the very thing that you dreaded." He crooked his mouth in a wry grimace. "I railroaded you into marrying me."

"Nick, I—"

"No, let me finish. For months I told you I understood your need to establish your independence, but in reality, I hoped to mold you into the wife I thought I wanted, that I needed."

"Nick, what kind of wife do you need me to be?" She waited as he stared out into the morning, his brow furrowed in thought. The sun breaking through the dissipating storm brought out the rich mahogany highlights in his ebony hair.

"Someone who is building a home, helping to raise our children. Someone who is there to support me when I need her." He returned his dark gaze to her. "Sounds old-fashioned, doesn't it? But that's what's important to me."

"You've just described the kind of husband I need. Were you planning on staying home to give me what I want?" She smiled at his startled expression, a sense of tenderness sweeping through her. "Don't you see, Nick? It doesn't matter whether I'm a working mother or a stay-at-home one. What counts is I'll be there for you and our children as you'll be there for me, no matter what."

"I can't ask for more, though I don't promise I might not revert to type now and then." He pulled her into his arms. "So what do you say. Shall we end this torment and start a real marriage?"

"Nick...Nick..." she murmured as she slipped her arms around his waist and buried her face in the hollow of his shoulder.

"Can I take this as a yes?" His voice held amusement as his warm breath stirred the hair at her temple.

"You certainly can...especially if you let me have my regular coffee again."

He chuckled as he caressed her upper arm. "I promise, you can drink regular coffee...after the baby's born."

She caught her breath as his expression changed from amusement to something more serious, something elemental.

He tunneled his fingers through her hair and brought her lips to his. This was a kiss of promise, the promise of a future forged with care and laughter and need. Leigh felt all the commitment from Nick she didn't hear in his vows at the wedding. Now she felt married, really married, and she used her mouth to show her pledge to him. The kiss spread heat like a healing balm through her, and her womb tightened as if the baby was celebrating their reunion. When he finally broke the kiss, she could hardly catch her breath.

He swiveled on the bed, nudging her with his hip to move over. He leaned back against the raised head of the bed, pulled her into his arms and urged her to put her head on his shoulder again.

"Okay, what's the first change on the schedule?" Leigh settled into his embrace with a satisfied sigh.

"Moving me into the bedroom?"

She tilted her head until she could see the grin on his face. "What kind of a pervert thinks of making love to a pregnant lady? A very pregnant lady?"

His mouth tempted hers again as he tightened his arms around her waist. "The kind of pervert who has missed the opportunity of holding his family safely through the night," he whispered against her lips.

"And we've missed you." She returned his hug, cherishing the security she had in his arms.

"No wonder our monitor signal is messed up. It wasn't designed to account for daddy sitting on the bed, holding mommy."

Leigh saw a nurse and Dr. Michaels standing in the doorway, a wide smile across his face.

"I knocked, but I guess you were . . . too busy to hear me," the doctor said as the nurse reset the IV machine, then left the room.

"Congratulate us," Nick announced. "We just decided to act married."

The doctor sat down in Nick's abandoned recliner and eyed Leigh's swollen stomach with an uplifted brow as Leigh punched Nick lightly in the ribs and glowered.

"What he means is...is..." As she looked at the amused physician, she knew there was no way she could explain. She pulled her dignity around her. "When can I go home?"

A stronger pain clenched her middle, and she gasped as she pressed back against Nick's arm. She looked questioningly at Dr. Michaels, and the older man nodded.

"The bleeding seems to have stopped but your labor has started again."

Nick's arm tightened around her shoulders. "Then you'll have to increase the medication again?"

Dr. Michaels rubbed his unshaven chin. "According to the lab, your baby's lungs are mature. I think it would be best to let this baby be born."

Leigh gasped as an upsurge of elation roared through her, mixed with fear. Nick's arm tightened around her, and she looked at him. He was watching her, his gaze loving, worried and yet somehow exultant.

"I wanted some change, but I didn't expect to start right off with the baby," he said with a laugh. He gestured to the calendar the night nurse had changed at midnight. "And August sixteenth is the perfect day for a birthday. Let's go for it. Are you ready, Mrs. Romano?"

"Yes." Suddenly there were no doubts, no fears. Just the overwhelming conviction that everything was right...for the first time since December. She raised her hand in a high-five sign. "Let's do it, Mr. Romano."

Epilogue

Leigh stripped the cellophane off the package of tinsel and carefully removed the silver strands from the cardboard backing. She peeled one strip after another from the metallic mass and laid it meticulously over a fragrant evergreen bough. After a few seconds she frowned, then sneaked a glance at the door. Good, Nick was still in the kitchen. What he didn't know wouldn't hurt her, she thought as she tossed several silvery strands onto the Christmas tree.

A soft gurgle of sound broke through the carols playing from the compact disc player and Leigh smiled as she eyed her four-month-old daughter, lying on her stomach in the playpen. Angela's widened eyes reflected the colors from the twinkling lights on the tree as she cooed at her mother, her tiny hand stretched outward.

"You're not going to tell on me, are you?" Leigh murmured. She stepped closer to the playpen and stroked the baby's velvet cheek, again marveling at Angela's downy, dark curls, so like Nick's. "I mean, so what if I don't lay the tinsel three inches on one side and the rest on the other side of the branch? Isn't it just as pretty my way, just sort of on there?''

The baby burbled, a wide toothless grin on her face. Her little arms and legs gyrated in her excitement, and Leigh laughed, her heart squeezing with love. How could she ever have thought to give away this wonderful gift?

Another song started on the player, and Leigh turned back to her job. She kept up her chatter with Angela as she continued tossing tinsel on the tree until it was gone.

''There, all done.'' She tilted her head and viewed the tree. On the half Nick had trimmed, the silver icicles flowed over the green branches like water, softening the dark green color. The other half of the tree showed the natural shade of the tree as the silvery strands connected the other decorations in an explosion of colors.

''Maybe he won't notice the difference.'' Leigh frowned in doubt, then turned to the baby. ''What do you think?''

''Trying to corrupt my daughter?'' Nick said from behind her. He handed Leigh a steaming mug of apple cider, then slipped his free hand around her waist. She took a sip of hot drink, savoring the spicy fragrance.

''Not corrupting her,'' Leigh said, her thoughts distracted as Nick's warm lips assaulted the sensitive area behind her ear. ''I'm showing her there is more than one option available to her when it comes to decorating Christmas trees.''

''How about if I show you some other options,'' he whispered, his apple-scented breath stirring the tendrils of hair at her nape.

He took her mug and placed it with his on an end table. He turned her to face him. She took one look at him and laughed. A woven circle of mistletoe rested on his tumbled dark curls. A wicked twinkle sparkled in his eyes.

''Wherever did you get that?''

''Never mind. Tradition says you owe me a kiss.''

''Gladly.'' She twined her arms around his neck, her insides melting at the thought of the taste of his mouth. ''But you don't need mistletoe. You'll never have to trick me into kissing you.''

His mouth fulfilled its promise—hot, wet and sweet. She gladly met the challenging duel with his tongue, and her knees weakened as his hands caressed her back, pulling her softness into his hard thighs. He groaned into her mouth, then tilted his head to deepen the kiss, and Leigh no longer heard the muted music, no longer smelled the sharp scent of evergreen. All she was conscious of was Nick, solid and loving in her arms.

He broke the kiss, his breathing heavy in her ear. ''Let's go into the bedroom and celebrate our anniversary.''

''What about...about...Angela?'' The sensation of Nick nibbling his way along her neck made it impossible for Leigh to focus on anything beyond the two of them.

Nick lifted his head long enough to glance toward the baby. ''I think she has worked out her own option.''

Leigh pulled free of her sensual haze and turned toward the playpen. Angela slept soundly, her soft lips slightly ajar. She smiled at the sight, her mother's heart melting as Nick gently covered the baby with a light blanket. His earlier words echoed in her mind.

''What anniversary are we supposed to be celebrating?''

''And they say women never forget anniversaries,'' Nick retorted as he straightened and placed his fists on his hips. ''The office Christmas party, where we started this little beauty, was a year ago today.''

Leigh realized he was correct. The past four months had been so wonderful, she had forgotten the pain and anguish of the early part of the year. She joined him by the sleeping baby and slid her arms around his waist, her curves fitting his angles perfectly. He grasped her hands as she rubbed her breasts against his chest.

He swept her up in his arms and headed for the bedroom. She clasped his shoulders, fighting to maintain her balance. ''Where are we going?'' she asked, her voice breathless.

''We're going to see if we can get us another Christmas bonus.''

She laughed and winked at the Christmas angel in red at the top of the tree.

*   *   *   *   *

MILLS & BOON®

Weddings ✤ *Glamour* ✤ *Family* ✤ *Heartbreak*

Weddings By DeWilde

Since the turn of the century, the elegant and fashionable DeWilde stores have helped brides around the world realise the fantasy of their 'special day'.

Now the store and three generations of the DeWilde family are torn apart by the separation of Grace and Jeffrey DeWilde—and family members face new challenges and loves in this fast-paced, glamourous, internationally set series.

For weddings, romance and glamour,
enter the world of

Weddings By DeWilde

—a fantastic line up of 12 new stories from popular Mills & Boon authors

NOVEMBER 1996

Bk. 3 DRESSED TO THRILL - Kate Hoffmann
Bk. 4 WILDE HEART - Daphne Clair

Available from WH Smith, John Menzies, Volume One, Forbuoys, Martins, Woolworths, Tesco, Asda, Safeway and other paperback stockists.

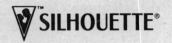

SILHOUETTE®

Dark Secrets...
Dangerous Desires

Lovers
DARK & DANGEROUS

Don't miss this superb three in one collection
featuring thrilling love stories with an edge of
darkness, suspense and paranormal, from some
of Silhouette's best-loved authors...

Heather Graham Pozzessere
Anne Stuart
Helen Myers

Available: October 1996   Price: £4.99

V™ SILHOUETTE

◈ SPECIAL EDITION ®

An invitation to three

from AMY FRAZIER

Marriages are made in Sweet Hope, Georgia—where the
brides and grooms-to-be are the last to find out!

♥   ♥   ♥   ♥   ♥

NEW BRIDE IN TOWN
October 1996

WAITING AT THE ALTAR
November 1996

A GOOD GROOM IS HARD TO FIND
December 1996

♥   ♥   ♥   ♥   ♥

SILHOUETTE
Desire

COMING NEXT MONTH

THE ACCIDENTAL BODYGUARD Ann Major

Man of the Month

The last thing lawyer Lucas Broderick wanted to do was protect the gorgeous woman he found hiding in his house. But she'd lost her memory…and now Lucas was losing his heart…

FATHER OF THE BROOD Elizabeth Bevarly

Sexy playboy Ike Guthrie reluctantly sold himself in a bachelor auction and was accidentally won by Annie Malone. Could the confirmed bachelor and the mother of a brood of children share more than a wild attraction?

THE GROOM, I PRESUME? Annette Broadrick

Daughters of Texas

Maribeth O'Brien was everything Chris Cochran wanted in a woman. So when she was left at the altar by her would-be groom, Chris stepped in to say, 'I do'!

FALCON'S LAIR Sara Orwig

Ben Falcon knew there was only one reason for a beautiful woman to have invaded his remote ranch. But until the mystery woman regained her memory, he could pretend she was someone he could trust - and that he was someone she could love…

HARDEN Diana Palmer

Texan Lovers

Rugged Harden Tremayne was the toughest, wildest man ever to come out of Texas. Miranda Warren had never felt anything as overwhelming as her passion for the long, lean cowboy. But was her love enough to melt his hard, hungry heart?

THE PRODIGAL GROOM Karen Leabo

The Wedding Night

Laurie Branson had been devastated when irresistible Jake Mercer left her at the altar. Now he was back—and that meant she had to keep a three-year-old secret she'd hidden since he left.

COMING NEXT MONTH FROM
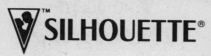 **SILHOUETTE**®

Sensation
A thrilling mix of passion, adventure and drama

UNCERTAIN ANGELS Kim Cates
ONE GOOD MAN Kathleen Creighton
CUTS BOTH WAYS Dee Holmes
SERIOUS RISKS Rachel Lee

Intrigue
Danger, deception and desire

RECKLESS LOVER Carly Bishop
EXPOSÉ Saranne Dawson
MIDNIGHT COWBOY Adrianne Lee
BABY VS. THE BAR M.J. Rodgers

Special Edition
Satisfying romances packed with emotion

PART-TIME WIFE Susan Mallery
THE REBEL'S BRIDE Christine Flynn
MARRIAGE-TO-BE? Gail Link
WAITING AT THE ALTAR Amy Frazier
RESIST ME IF YOU CAN Janis Reams Hudson
LONESOME COWBOY Lois Faye Dyer

To celebrate the **1000**th Desire™ title we're giving away a year's supply of Silhouette Desire® novels — absolutely *FREE!*

All you have to do is complete the puzzle below and send it to us by 31 December 1996.

The first 10 correct entries drawn from the bag will each win 12 month's free supply of seductive and breathtaking Silhouette Desire books (6 books every month—worth over £160). The second correct 10 entries drawn will each win a Silhouette music cassette.

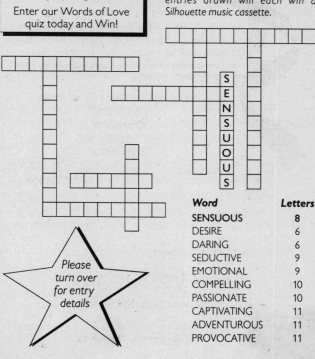

Word	Letters
SENSUOUS	8
DESIRE	6
DARING	6
SEDUCTIVE	9
EMOTIONAL	9
COMPELLING	10
PASSIONATE	10
CAPTIVATING	11
ADVENTUROUS	11
PROVOCATIVE	11

Please turn over for entry details

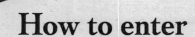

CELEBRATION 1000

How to enter

There are ten words listed overleaf, each of which fits into spaces in the grid according to their length. All you have to do is fit the correct word into the appropriate spaces that have been provided for its letters. We've even done the first one for you!

When you have completed the grid, don't forget to fill in your name and address in the space provided below and pop this page into an envelope (you don't even need a stamp) and post it today. Hurry—competition ends 31st December 1996.

**Silhouette® Words of Love
FREEPOST
Croydon
Surrey
CR9 3WZ**

Are you a Reader Service Subscriber?   Yes ❏   No ❏

Ms/Mrs/Miss/Mr _____

Address _____

_____

_____ Postcode _____

One application per household.

You may be mailed with other offers from other reputable companies as a result of this application. If you would prefer not to receive such offers, please tick box. ❏

mps MAILING PREFERENCE SERVICE   DMA

SILC96